CHERRY AMES NURSE STORIES

CHERRY AMES VISITING NURSE

By

HELEN WELLS

Springer Publishing Company, LLC
11 West 42nd Street, 15th Floor
New York, NY 10036-8002

Acquisitions Editor: Sally J. Barhydt
Production Editor: Matthew Byrd
Cover design by Takeout Graphics, Inc.
Composition: Techbooks

17 18 19 20 / 4 3 2 1

Library of Congress Cataloging-in-Publication Data

Wells, Helen, 1910-
Cherry Ames, visiting nurse / by Helen Wells.
p. cm.— (Cherry Ames nurse stories)
Summary: Cherry reunites with her old Spencer classmates when they all decide to take an apartment together and work for the Visiting Nurse Service of New York.
ISBN 0-8261-0399-5
[1. Nurses—Fiction. 2. New York (N.Y.)–History–1898-1951–Fiction.]
I. Title.

PZ7.W4644Cn 2006
[Fic]—dc22

2006022321

Printed in the United States of America by Gasch Printing

Contents

	Foreword	v
I	Fresh Start	1
II	The Spencer Club	16
III	The Visiting Nurses	35
IV	Ann to the Rescue	46
V	Tryout	68
VI	Cherry's Own District	85
VII	The Mysterious Mansion	101
VIII	Parties and Clues	126
IX	Unknown Neighbors	138
X	In Hiding	149
XI	The Secret	165
XII	A Welcome Guest	184
XIII	The Test	199
XIV	Christmas Party	213

Foreword

Helen Wells, the author of the Cherry Ames stories, said, "I've always thought of nursing, and perhaps you have, too, as just about the most exciting, important, and rewarding, profession there is. Can you think of any other skill that is *always* needed by everybody, everywhere?"

I was and still am a fan of Cherry Ames. Her courageous dedication to her patients; her exciting escapades; her thirst for knowledge; her intelligent application of her nursing skills; and the respect she achieved as a registered nurse (RN) all made it clear to me that I was going to follow in her footsteps and become a nurse—nothing else would do. Thousands of other young people were motivated by Cherry Ames to become RNs as well. Cherry Ames motivated young people on into the 1970s, when the series ended. Readers who remember reading these books in the past will enjoy rereading them now—whether or not they chose nursing as a career—and perhaps sharing them with others.

My career has been a rich and satisfying one, during which I have delivered babies, saved lives, and cared for people in hospitals and in their homes. I have worked at the bedside and served as an administrator. I have published journals, written articles, taught students, consulted, and given expert testimony. Never once did I regret my decision to enter nursing.

During the time I was publishing a nursing journal, I became acquainted with Robert Wells, brother of Helen Wells. In the course of conversation I learned that Ms. Wells had passed on and left the Cherry Ames copyright to Mr. Wells. Because there is a shortage of nurses here in the US today, I thought, "Why not bring Cherry back to motivate a whole new generation of young people? Why not ask Mr. Wells for the copyright to Cherry Ames?" Mr. Wells agreed, and the republished series is dedicated both to Helen Wells, the original author, and to her brother, Robert Wells, who transferred the rights to me. I am proud to ensure the continuation of Cherry Ames into the twenty-first century.

The final dedication is to you, both new and old readers of Cherry Ames: It is my dream that you enjoy Cherry's nursing skills as well as her escapades. I hope that young readers will feel motivated to choose nursing as their life's work. Remember, as Helen Wells herself said: there's no other skill that's "*always* needed by everybody, everywhere."

Harriet Schulman Forman, RN, EdD
Series Editor

CHAPTER I

Fresh Start

IT WAS A HOT AFTERNOON AT THE END OF AUGUST. THE whole Midwest town of Hilton looked wilted. Even this tree-shaded block, and the Ameses' big, gray frame house and lawn, wore a dusty, tail-end-of-summer look. Cherry, sitting forlorn on the porch steps, debated whether the long summer ever would be over.

"Of course, summer is my favorite season," she argued to herself. "But I've had enough of doing nothing. What I want is a new fall hat and new, exciting things to do!" She wrinkled her nose as if trying to detect any first autumn briskness in the air.

The hot breeze carried to her only the scent of over-ripe greenery. Cherry sighed and pushed her black curls off her forehead, off the back of her too-warm neck. She fanned her red cheeks, muttering, "Where, oh, where is that mailman?"

For any mail delivery, any day now, would tell her whether or not she was to go to New York this fall, and become a visiting nurse. Cherry had already sent in her application for the job—including transcripts of her R.N. degree from Spencer Nursing School, her record as an Army nurse, as a private duty nurse, and a glowing personal reference from Dr. Joseph Fortune.

She supposed that the other nurses from her own Spencer School crowd were awaiting the mailman just as eagerly as she was. If their applications to become visiting nurses were accepted, several of the girls were to take an apartment together in New York.

The screen door opened and Mrs. Ames came out on the flower-vined porch. She was a pretty, dark-eyed woman, slim and youthful looking. She hesitated on the top step.

"Still waiting for the mail, Cherry?"

Cherry stood up. "Still waiting. I feel like Poor Butterfly, or a mislaid umbrella. You look so warm, Mother—almost as warm as I feel. Shall I make some lemonade?"

Edith Ames walked over to the swing and sat down. "No, thanks, dear. Unless you want some yourself. At least, this heat is good for the late crops. And for my dahlias."

Cherry grinned. "Your pet dahlias!" Her mother struggled with them every late summer and fall.

Mrs. Ames stiffened slightly. "You know my dahlias always win Hilton's Garden Club ribbon." Suddenly she grinned too, and her face was as merry as Cherry's. "Nurse, my dahlias are to me what your patients are to you!"

Cherry and her mother nodded at each other in perfect understanding.

A voice boomed from somewhere in the house:

"Did I hear someone mention refreshments?"

It was Cherry's twin brother, Charlie, who had recently been released from the Army Air Forces. Mrs. Ames reported to Cherry that Charlie had just taken his fourth shower of the day, had raided the icebox so continuously that she was kept busy refilling it, and that Charlie, too, was waiting for the mailman.

Cherry nodded. "For his notice from State Engineering College."

"Yes. Dad and I do want Charles to go back and finish his schooling." Mrs. Ames fell to musing. "The war interrupted all our lives, didn't it?"

"Well, here's one candidate for a fresh start," Cherry said cheerfully. "Gosh, how I hope the Visiting Nurse Service writes back *yes*. Yes to all us Spencer hopefuls." She thought how awful it would be if any one of the girls was turned down, left out.

The screen door flew open and Charlie strode out on the porch. He was a tall, athletic young man, fair-haired and light-eyed. The Ames twins looked like a negative and a print of the same picture: identical, lively faces, but Charlie blond and Cherry vividly dark.

He grinned at their mother and sat down beside Cherrry on the porch steps.

"I'm the cleanest," he announced. "Undoubtedly the coolest."

Cherry sniffed. "You've been using my sandalwood soap."

"Horrors, did I? I'll have to take another shower, then. How's the mailman situation?" Charlie put his arm across Cherry's shoulders and started to sing, in a passable baritone, "Waitin'—yes, just waitin'—awaitin' for the evenin' mail!"

Cherry chimed in. They sang three choruses, if not well, at least enthusiastically. Mrs. Ames shook her head.

"Don't you care for our singing, madam?"

"It is so harmonious I can hardly tear myself away. But I will." Mrs. Ames smiled at them and vanished into the house.

"Look! Gaze yonder!" Charlie flung out a sunburned arm and pointed. "Blue-coated figure doth approach!"

"Gadzooks!" Cherry responded, shading her eyes. "It is ye mailman or I'll be a two-headed, brindle cow."

"Please don't be a cow," Charlie requested earnestly. "I think you're prettier the way you are. C'mon, Sis, let's go meet him."

Her brother yanked her to her feet and they went loping together across the grass. Charlie soon outdistanced her. "Slowpoke," he called over his shoulder.

"Only because you're taller than I am," Cherry puffed indignantly.

"Excuses, nothing but excuses."

Charlie reached the mailman first. He came strolling back to Cherry with a fistful of letters.

"No, yours didn't come yet, honey. But here's a letter from State Engineering College for me!"

"Here's hoping," Cherry said loyally.

Charlie ripped the envelope open and held the letter so they could read it together. The college notified Charles Ames that he had been accepted for continuation of his course of study, broken off when he enlisted, and that he might matriculate the week after Labor Day.

"Charlie, that's wonderful!" Cherry exclaimed.

"Only two weeks off," Charlie said thoughtfully. He looked worriedly at his sister. "Wish your plans were settled, too."

"I'll come out all right," she said, and meant it. "Meanwhile, congratulations! And good luck toward winning your degree!" She grinned at her twin. "You're bursting to go show Mother that letter, and call up Dad, aren't you? Well, go ahead."

"Want to write Bucky Hall about it, too! Excuse me!" And Charlie raced off.

Cherry followed him, twisting off a marigold and chewing its stem. She was glad for her brother. She half wished the Ames twins might be going to school together again. But Charlie's career lay in aerial engineering, and hers in nursing. Cherry tossed back her black curls. Well, she would just have to see her adored brother on vacations and holidays.

Nevertheless, she could not help feeling a bit forlorn. Maybe it was this waiting. Cherry was too restless and active a person to wait comfortably. She told herself to stop fretting and enjoy her leisure, enforced though it was.

Back in the house, she wandered around the mahogany-and-blue living room. Cherry was fond of this hospitable room which had held so many parties. In the dining room beyond stood the big family table and the sunny bay window filled with fresh, green plants. She found the big, white kitchen deserted, an apple pie cooling on the table. A piece had already been cut out of it—Charlie! She could hear him and their mother talking in the garden. Cherry smiled, fished a chunk of apple out of the pie, popped it in her mouth, and went along upstairs, up the wide, Victorian staircase.

At the top of the stairs, before the open door of her own room, she stood thinking. She could redecorate her room. That would be fun. But it was a big job and she might be called away to New York with only two walls repainted and the draperies down.

"I hope! Besides, I like my little red-and-white room the way it is." She looked affectionately at the dressing table with its saucy, starched skirts, tied back with broad, red ribbons. "Might go give little Midge a hand, if she wants it."

Midge Fortune needed all the assistance Cherry could give her, just now when she had to start back to high school in two weeks. Motherless Midge lived with her doctor-scientist father, the absent-minded Dr. Joe, and kept house for him, after a fashion. Attending high school and running the cottage was a double job for a young girl. It did not faze Midge, however, who could blithely serve up peanut butter sandwiches and call it dinner, and just as blithely forget to do her algebra homework.

Cherry would have chuckled at Midge's happy-go-lucky methods except for one thing. Elderly Dr. Joe had not been well ever since the Army Medical Corps discharged him from medical research. He protested that he was quite all right, and went ahead with his work at Hilton clinic, and puttered until all hours in his homemade laboratory. But it seemed to Cherry that Dr. Fortune was crawling about his tasks, on will power rather than energy. She was concerned, for Dr. Joe was both her charge and her mentor. Through his teachings and his inspiring example, Cherry had come to her beloved profession of nursing. The least she could do for him, now, was to see that Midge kept him nourished.

"If I'm off to New York, I'll have to keep after Midge by letter," Cherry thought as she went down the stairs and left the house. Turning off her block, she crossed to Pine Street and walked down another quiet, leafy street.

She waved to Kitty Loomis, who was sitting on the porch of her red-brick house, sewing. Kitty ran down to tell Cherry she had just been graduated from nursing school, and was going to Chicago to take her first nursing job.

"That's wonderful, Kitty! I know you'll do well."

"And what are you going to do, Cherry?"

"Why—uh—" Cherry gulped. "My nursing plans are still unsettled. I'll have to let you know."

"Please do," Kitty said. "Write me at Heath Hospital in Chicago—because I'm leaving Hilton September first."

September first! Cherry shook her head as she waved to Kitty and went along toward the Fortunes' street. Suppose—just suppose—the Visiting Nurse Service rejected her? What *would* she do next? Then she caught herself sharply. "Stop enjoying your misery," she counseled herself. "In the first place, nothing has gone wrong—yet. In the second place, a registered nurse is always needed and can always find interesting work to do. Hmm, not very cheering, is it?"

The flagstone path to the Fortunes' small, white cottage was neatly cleared of weeds, the windows shone, and the winter draperies aired on the clothesline behind the hollyhocks. That was Cherry and Midge's handiwork. Cherry had persuaded Midge to get the Fortune household in apple-pie order before the high school term started.

Cherry rapped on the open front door. No one answered. She went in.

"Midge?" she called.

Through the small sitting room, Cherry could see into the laboratory. It was empty: Dr. Joe was still downtown at the clinic. Cherry went out to the kitchen, on the chance that Midge, newly zealous from Cherry's prodding, might be preparing dinner. No Midge. The girl's bedroom was deserted, too, with every garment and cold cream jar Midge owned flung around the little room in glorious confusion.

"Midge!" she called. "Miss Margaret Fortune! You must be home, with the front door standing wide open!"

A faint, strangled shout from the garage answered her. Cherry went back there. There, safely out of the neighbors' view, was Midge in a bathing suit, face oily with cream, light-brown hair in pigtails, standing shakily on her hands. The teen-ager was the oddest sight Cherry had seen in a long time. Midge waved one foot in greeting.

"Midge, in heaven's name, what are you doing?"

Midge's upside down, flushed, sticky face contrived to grin at her. "Gebbing—broofoo," Midge choked.

"What?"

Midge wobbled, toppled and fell. One hand landed on an opened magazine. She held it up, brightly indicating the beauty advice page. "I said, I'm getting beautiful. Standing on your head is the best thing in the world for your circulation."

Cherry rubbed one rosy cheek and stared. "Is anything wrong with your circulation?"

"Oh, no. But I want that glowing look."

"You're glowing, all right. You look like a boiled lobster."

"'The anti-wrinkle cream,'" Midge read, unruffled, from the magazine, "'is doubly effective when the circulation is stimulated. Massage the wrinkles lightly—'"

"You won't have wrinkles for another thirty or forty years!"

"This is preventive. A girl can't start too soon."

Cherry burst out laughing. Her dark eyes danced. "You remind me of the time I put a mud pack on my face and it hardened and I couldn't get it off for six hours. Charlie threatened to use a hammer. Incidentally, Miss Fortune, why must you make a spectacle of yourself in the garage, of all places?"

"'Always exercise in the open air if possible,'" Midge read virtuously from the beauty advice page. She waved at the open garage door. "Oodles of fresh air. Besides, no one can see me back here, behind these hollyhocks and the clothesline."

That was true.

"Also," continued Midge, "I won't have time for self-improvement once high school starts. It's only two weeks away."

Those dates again. Cherry sighed. Everyone had definite plans for the fall and winter but herself. She asked Midge, rather warningly, what she planned to serve Dr. Joe for dinner this evening. Midge hoisted herself on hands and head once more, and replied:

"Gloop."

"Soup?"

"At's w'at I'ed—gloop."

Cherry seized Midge by the ankles and turned her right side up. The teen-ager's hazel eyes turned dark gray in annoyance.

"Now you listen to me!" Cherry exclaimed, trying not to laugh. "Your poor dad needs better meals than *gloop*, young lady. Suppose both of you have dinner with us tonight."

Cherry knew no special permission from her mother was needed. Midge had practically grown up in the Ames household.

That evening the Fortunes sat down with the Ameses around the big table. Cherry's father, serving at the head of the table, was an older, graying, but still handsome version of his blond son. Dr. Joe, in his accustomed chair, seemed small and tired tonight. One lock of gray hair, as usual, stubbornly fell in his eye and, as usual, Dr. Joe abstractedly kept pushing it back.

"Well, Cherry, did the mailman remember you today?" Mr. Ames asked.

"Not yet, Will, and did you," Mrs. Ames countered brightly, "ah—remember to buy me a new pair of garden shears?"

"What garden shears?" Mr. Ames scowled. "Edith, I don't understand you! And I don't understand why Cherry didn't hear—"

"Oh, dear, I've dropped my fork," Mrs. Ames exclaimed, dropping it. "Midge dear, will you get me another?"

Cherry and Charlie exchanged grins. There was a trace of concern in her brother's face. Cherry said:

"Announcement. I haven't heard about my application. Anybody who wishes to remark on it, may do so. I feel gloomy, anyway."

Dr. Fortune glanced up. "No cause for gloom, my dear," he said absently. "You can always stay here in Hilton and nurse for me."

"That's right!" Mr. Ames said firmly. "I was thinking it's time Cherry stopped traipsing around and stayed at home for a change. Brush up on her cooking. Learn to sew. Be a help to her mother."

"Feed the cat," said Charlie, straight-faced. "Water the plants. Never see anyone but the grocer, and go to bed at eight o'clock."

"No nursing? Horrors!" Cherry exclaimed.

Next morning, Saturday, brought a letter from Gwen Jones, Cherry's old classmate. It was postmarked from Gwen's home town in Pennsylvania. "I've been accepted! Bertha writes from their farm that the Visiting Nurse Service of New York has accepted her, too. I'm going straight to New York and find us an apartment. How does Greenwich Village strike you as a location for us?"

"'Us,'" Cherry thought mournfully. "Oh, well. I can always visit the girls. Or something."

The Saturday noon delivery brought a note from Mai Lee, the Chinese-American girl Cherry had trained and worked with. "Just heard from the Visiting Nurse Service and they not only said yes! They really want me, because I can speak two or three words of Chinese. Suppose they will assign me to Chinatown for my territory. When will *you* arrive in New York, Cherry?"

It was awful. Sunday was worse, for there was no mail on Sunday. Monday was Labor Day, and deadly dull.

Tuesday morning brought an advertisement, a bill, an exultant letter from another old classmate and friend, Vivian Warren, a postcard from Josie Franklin marked simply "Hurray!" and a cool, driving rain.

"At least, it's a fall rain," thought Cherry. "Guess I'd better do my room over, after all. Guess I'll go hide out at the movies this afternoon." Everyone else was too busy to go with her.

Cherry sat through two features, a newsreel, and a cartoon without clearly seeing any of them. When she emerged from the movie theater, the rain had stopped and the air was fresh and tangy. On Main Street she saw purple grapes and frosty-cheeked plums in the fruiterer's window.

And when she reached home, there was a letter awaiting her! Someone, Charlie probably, had tied it to a long, red ribbon and hung it from the living-room chandelier, so Cherry would be sure to see it. The letter swung festively and tantalizingly out of her reach—Charlie had made sure of that.

Breathless with excitement, Cherry dragged a chair over and climbed up on it. She glanced at the envelope—yes, it was *the* one. Then she noticed on the envelope that the letter mistakenly had been addressed to Hilton, Indiana, had traveled all the way back to New York, and then had been readdressed to Hilton, Illinois, mailed once more, and finally reached her. So that was the cause for the delay! She tore the letter open.

"—accepted—visiting nurse—please report in New York before September tenth, if possible—"

"If possible!" Cherry laughed for joy. She teetered on the chair in sheer excitement.

Charlie's tow head carefully emerged from the hall, and her mother's sympathetic face peered in from the dining room.

"Is everything all right?" they breathed.

"Everything is perfect!" Cherry crowed. "Marvelous —perfect—I'm going to New York, think of that—!"

She tumbled off the chair and sat on the floor where she landed, laughing up at her relieved family.

CHAPTER II

The Spencer Club

"THIS CAN'T BE IT!" CHERRY SAID.

The taxi driver turned around. "Look, lady. You give me an address, did'n' ya? I ain't responsible for this here crazy Greenwich Village."

Cherry alighted. She peered around, delighted and astonished, at the narrow crooked street and the ancient, little brick houses.

"Seventy-five cents, lady."

"Oh! Here you are." She paid him, then reached into the cab for her suitcase.

The taxi driver looked skeptically at the ten-cent tip she had given him. Then he studied Cherry, fresh-faced and trim, in her red suit and tiny black hat perched on her black curls.

"Look, lady. You ain't the Village type. You shoulda stood in Brooklyn. Like me."

"What's the Village type?" she asked, startled.

"You'll find out," the taxi driver promised. He drove off, narrowly missing two small urchins chasing a beribboned cat.

Cherry, mystified, took a careful look at this street. Nothing ominous here! These demure little houses from Revolutionary days had crisp curtains and white shutters at their many-paned windows. Their brass doorposts gleamed brightly in the sun. Window boxes of geranium and ivy made splashes of color all up and down the little street.

"Now what did that driver mean?"

Cherry picked up her suitcase and mounted two steps from the sidewalk into No. 9. The ground floor of this house was to be theirs, Gwen had written.

In a pleasantly dim hallway, Cherry found a mahogany table piled with mail for several tenants, a bowl of fresh flowers, a carpeted stairway winding upstairs, and a blue door. Beside the doorbell was tacked a neat row of engraved cards: Gwenthyan Jones R.N., Mai Lee R.N., Vivian L. Warren R.N. Bertha Larsen and Josie Franklin had their cards up, too. Cherry fished out her own professional card and propped it in with the others. Then she rang the doorbell, long and lustily.

A scowling, red-haired girl pulled the door open. She had a smudge of paint across her puckish, freckled face, and a row of nails stuck in the belt of her overalls. Her scowl disappeared when she saw Cherry.

"Cherry!" Gwen cried. "What a relief to see someone

who doesn't hate me!" Two sturdy arms, hardware, and Wet paint smudge landed around Cherry. "The late Miss Ames! I thought you were never coming!"

"I thought so myself," Cherry confessed. She beamed at Gwen Jones. "Aren't you going to let me in?"

"No," said Gwen, the scowl returning. She closed the door and pushed Cherry back into the hall. "Ssh. Listen. You've got to be on my side!"

"What's wrong? Who's on the other side?"

"You'll hear about it soon enough from the others," Gwen said glumly. "Oh, golly, are we in an uproar! Cherry, for heaven's sakes, speak up for me! After all, I did this—"

"Did what?"

The blue door jerked open and a large, plump, fair girl glared at Gwen.

"The kitchen is little and I am big. You knew I would be the cook. And the stove has only one heat: feeble. Hello, Cherry."

"Hello, Bertha," Cherry stammered. She had never before seen Bertha Larsen angry. "How are you?"

"I am disgusted. Come in and see what Gwen rented. It is more homelike in the chicken coop on our farm."

Cherry and a disgruntled Gwen followed the big girl into the living room. Assorted chairs and tables were pushed around, the windows were bare of curtains, and the girls' half-unpacked belongings were strewn everywhere.

"It's not so bad," Cherry said, bright and hollow.

"Look at the gold-and-white sprigged wallpaper. Look at the fireplace. Uh—look at—"

A large sob from another room interrupted her.

"Josie Franklin is already homesick," Gwen snorted.

Bertha quashed the redhead with a glance. "What Josie saw is enough to give anybody a turn."

Cherry was by now thoroughly bewildered. She saw nothing so far to make Josie cry. She went off down a narrow hallway, found three tiny double bedrooms, and Josie Franklin in the last one.

Josie sat ostensibly weeping over a newspaper. It was opened at the obituary column. She glanced up from behind her glasses at Cherry.

"Look!" Josie pointed a shaking finger. "Dead. Josephine Franklin. Me! My name—right there—Ohhh!"

"Josie dear, it's not you," Cherry struggled not to laugh at Josie's clowning. "It's somebody else with the same name. You're not dead."

"But I don't want my name in the dead column! It makes me nervous. A fine welcome to New York!"

Cherry pretended to comfort her until Josie gave up the joke and assumed her usual rabbity expression. Suddenly she wailed:

"It's all Gwen's fault!"

"Poor Gwen. *What* is her fault?"

"Greenwich Village. Of all awful places!" This time there was real woe in Josie's voice.

Cherry ruefully remembered the taxi driver and kept quiet. With relief she heard someone calling her.

It was Vivian Warren, a fragile, pretty girl, running down the long hall and buttoning herself up the back. Cherry ran to meet her halfway.

"Well, hello!" They exchanged hugs. Vivian's soft, hazel eyes glowed, and her fine, pale skin flushed with pleasure. "Cherry, I hated missing the girls' reunion at your house this summer."

"It was fun—forming the Spencer Club and planning this visiting nurse thing. We missed you too, Vivi."

"I was working," Vivian said with a little sigh.

As usual, Cherry thought. She felt again the old surge of protectiveness for Vivian, just as when she had come to the girl's rescue in their nursing school days. Vivian's family was too poor to help her, and she had had a lonely struggle.

"Vivi, you're entirely too thin," Cherry said. "We're all going to feed you and fatten you up."

"Hear, hear! Want to help paint bookcases? I was, but I got so tired and dirty, even Gwen relented. That slave driver."

Cherry's answer was lost in a roar. Three fire engines raced past their windows. A fresh wail came from Josie. Upstairs someone started to sing scales.

"—wich Village," Vivian shouted, fingers in her ears. "Gwen's idea—"

Cherry began to see what Gwen Jones was talking about. She also began to see the other girls' point. And she had not seen the Village itself, so far. What had Gwen led the Spencer Club into?

And what were Gwen, Bertha and Josie staring at, out the living room window, faces frozen in disbelief?

Cherry and Vivian squeezed in among them and stared too. Crossing the street came a barefoot man in flowing white toga and flowing white beard. He carried a staff and looked utterly unconcerned.

"Who's that?" Bertha gasped. "Moses?"

Gwen gulped. "Uh—why—he's a famous dancer or something. Lives down here. You know, lots of artists live down here in the Village."

"Then what are people like us doing here?" Vivian demanded.

Gwen looked crosser than ever. "I've explained and explained. There are twenty everyday folks to one Bohemian around here. The Village isn't only an art center. It's a small, friendly *village* in the heart of New York. Why, we even have a garden."

"We have?" Cherry exclaimed loyally. She tossed back her black curls. "I must see it."

"Down the hall and don't fall through the trap door," Josie said gloomily.

Cherry sped off. She passed the three bedrooms, went through a dismantled back parlor, and out a back door. But this was no garden by Cherry's definition. It was a tiny square of grass enclosed by a high, board fence, with a solid row of tall, brick houses looking down on it.

"It feels like being at the bottom of a well," Cherry thought uncomfortably. "Still, it's something green, it's outdoors." It even had two city sparrows.

She spied a knothole in the fence and was drawn irresistibly to peek through. In the neighbor's minuscule yard stood a few straggly stalks of corn. Cherry giggled: on her prairies, corn grew eight feet high, by the hundreds of miles.

"Wonder if they keep a cow, too." She ran back into the house, calling to Gwen for the benefit of the others: "The garden is—er—really a find, in a city of stone and steel. We can even have meals out there."

Gwen looked grateful. But the others looked grumpy and did not deign to reply. Cherry changed the subject.

"Where's Mai Lee all this time?"

"Out marketing. Oh! Did you know that Ann Evans—sorry, Mrs. Jack Powell—is living right here in New York too? Ann hasn't seen this—this lunatic rattrap yet."

Gwen shouted: "The Village is romantic!"

The others pounced on her. Bertha declared she would take "less atmosphere and a decent kitchen!" Cherry saw that something had to be done—someone had to come to Gwen's rescue—before a real quarrel broke out. She said hastily, "Let's see the kitchen, Bertha."

Down the hall, crammed into a converted closet, was a small stove, miniature icebox, tiny sink. Shelves were built into whatever inches were left. Cherry whistled. Bertha snorted. Gwen quietly sneaked off.

"Space is very precious in New York." Cherry tried to smooth things over.

Fortunately the doorbell rang then.

"Must be Mai Lee," Vivian said, starting to go.

"Let me go!" Cherry said.

She by-passed the packing box and a fairly respectable sofa, and pulled open the blue door. There stood two immense, brown paper bags of groceries, clutched by two ivory hands, and apparently walking on a pair of neat, silk-stockinged legs. Cherry laughed and reached for the paper bags. Mai Lee's demure face emerged, badly scared.

"Ch-Cherry! Hello!"

"Hello, dear—but have you seen a ghost?"

The other girls crowded around. Mai Lee emptied change from her pocket onto the packing box, and pushed back her satiny black hair.

"I met a tiger on the sidewalk," Mai Lee panted.

"That's the Village," Gwen said brightly. "Always something exotic."

"Very exotic to have him try to nip my ankle." The little Chinese-American girl gingerly stuck out her ankle. "It's a good thing he was a baby and on a leash. A blonde woman had him, she looked like an actress."

"Probably was," Gwen said airily. "Isn't it fascinating to go out marketing and meet celebrities?"

"No!" they thundered at her.

Cherry waved her arms in desperation. "Let's open the groceries! Let's have lunch!" Anything to keep peace, even if only temporarily.

Lunch accomplished a truce. The girls fished eagerly in the paper bags, approving the pickles especially. Cherry took a moment to ask Mai Lee about Marie Swift.

"Yes, Marie and I got together in San Francisco, while I was out there visiting my family," Mai Lee said as she ripped open a box of potato chips. Marie, one of their original Spencer School crowd, had decided to remain with her mother, who was undergoing a long illness. "Marie really is disappointed that she can't join us," Mai Lee reported. "I promised her we'd send her bulletins from time to time."

"And snapshots," said Vivian. "I brought my camera." She held out a parcel of cold cuts. "Who wants samples?"

They perched on the packing box and on the few lone pieces of furniture, and had a sort of picnic lunch. After eating they were in a better temper, but not for long.

There came a pounding from somewhere below. The girls searched frantically, and finally remembered the trap door in the hall. When they unlatched it, up popped a gnarled little man, the janitor. He crawled through and demanded:

"Why didn't ye answer? I've been pounding a good five minutes!"

"Why didn't you use the regular door?" Gwen retorted.

"Because I'm testing this here door, Miss Smarty! Goin' to nail it down," and he started banging away.

"Miss Smarty," repeated Josie under her breath.

"Stop that!" The redhead whirled on her.

"Truce, truce!" Cherry waved her white handkerchief. "Now, look, kids. The apartment isn't so bad. We can fix it up. You haven't even tried, all you've done is gripe—"

"Cherry's right," Vivian said loyally over the janitor's banging. "We can fix it to suit ourselves—"

The janitor stopped hammering to say tartly, "Ye'll do no fixing without my permission. Remember this here is a rented place. The stuff in it ain't yours, Miss Smarty!"

Vivian and Cherry shepherded the girls into the back parlor while the janitor finished his hammering. This room, with windows facing the garden, was not bad. It was square and good-sized and flooded with September sunshine.

"We could make it into a dining room and a sort of study room," Bertha Larsen admitted.

"But these wooden chairs and table are so dreary," Mai Lee said. "And battered! Good for kindling."

"Paint 'em," Cherry said impulsively. "Bright blue for fun. And—um—we could paper the room. With one of those red, white, and blue Pennsylvania Dutch papers." Cherry's black eyes sparkled. "You know, funny little formalized people and birds. Not expensive, either."

Everyone looked happier, and Bertha Larsen nodded approval. A gleam came into her china-blue eyes.

"I'll go right away and buy the paint," she announced. "Then we can paint tomorrow. Because once we report to our jobs on Monday, we won't have much time to paint." She added emphatically, "I like Cherry's idea of painting. It is the only good idea we've had."

"We daren't paint without the janitor's permission!" they warned.

"He will say yes," Bertha answered stubbornly. "Anybody would be glad to have clean paint on that awful old furniture."

"Wait till we get his permission!"

Bertha grumbled and stalked out of the room. The other girls shook their heads. Big Bertha was usually motherly and patient, almost phlegmatic. She must feel exceedingly disappointed about the apartment to be so cross and stubborn now. In a way, Cherry could not blame Bertha. But they had a lease and could not move, so it behooved them to make the place livable.

Cherry looked out into the hall. The janitor, that terrible little man, had vanished. In a body, prodded by Cherry, the girls moved into the front living room. They settled down to a conference on decorating, excepting Bertha, who was doing some chores in the kitchen.

There were a few black looks at Gwen, and a few peppery remarks in return. But the Spencer Club, still prodded by Cherry, began to do something constructive.

"Now, this front room has possibilities," Vivian pointed out. "It isn't so much a question of what furniture you have, as how invitingly you can arrange it."

There was only a couch, two chairs, and a few small tables. But the carpet was passable and the gold-and-white wallpaper really attractive. The fireplace was handsome. Under Vivian's direction, they collected all the furniture in the apartment except the beds and studied it.

Then they grouped chairs on either side of the stately fireplace, dragged the couch to the opposite wall, and set low tables within easy reach. On the far wall they placed tall, twin chests of drawers, robbing Cherry and Gwen's bedroom but with good effect.

"It looks better," they agreed, heartened. They set Gwen's low bookcases under the street windows. "Let's get yellow curtains to pick up the gold sprig in the wallpaper. Thin, gold gauze curtains."

"Made very full," Mai Lee suggested. "We can make them ourselves. It's only hemming."

"We need more lamps," Cherry fretted. "Yes, Gwen told me she is having a couple of lamps shipped from home. But even so—"

"Well, if we make the curtains, we'll be able to afford lamps. Crystal ones, maybe." Gwen was daring to assert herself again. "We can paint the bookcases pale yellow, too."

"I want plants," Josie insisted. "And framed photographs of our families and friends all over."

"And a silver tea service? Certainly."

It took them almost all afternoon. But everyone felt better now. Peace—a rather gingerly peace—was achieved.

Cherry saw incipient danger signals in the tired droop of Vivian's slender figure and in Josie's "hungry" look. To avert trouble, she suggested:

"We're all too tired to cook. Let's go out to dinner."

"Yes, it would be fun to explore," Mai Lee seconded. "Incidentally, where's Bertha?"

They found her, stubborn and not talking, in the tiny bedroom she shared with Josie. She was putting her clothes away and refused to come out to dinner.

"I don't want to get dressed up. I'll have something here."

"Me too," Gwen said, plucking at her overalls. "I'll stay with you, Bertha."

"No!" said Bertha.

The others more or less defended Gwen, justified her taking the apartment, and said quite firmly that it was time for Bertha to relent. Bertha did not unbend.

"She doesn't love me," Gwen sighed. "Okay, kids, I'll take a fast shower and be ready in five minutes."

Out they started, cleaned up, hatted, and gloved

as befitting a city street. They felt heartless at leaving Bertha alone, and inexplicably uneasy about her. But they also felt quite elegant, dining out in New York.

Eagerly the five girls went along their street, glimpsing lighted windows and handsome apartments. Traffic sounds came softly from the big thoroughfares a few blocks away. Cherry saw a domed Byzantine church tower and flocks of pigeons wheeling in the violet sky: it all looked like an etching at this twilight hour.

Turning a corner, they encountered an orderly stream of men and women coming home after the day's work. Cherry wondered if the taxi driver had not been prejudiced against the Village—"a Brooklyn patriot."

A block farther on, there was more traffic, more people and shops. Cherry's eyes bugged out at the Eighth Street shops. Here were elephant-hide fans from India, bright serapes from Mexico, topazes from Brazil, books from France, a windowful of grotesque masks, another window displaying a single, beautiful sculpture banked in rhododendron leaves.

"Look! Lots of people just like ourselves," Gwen was saying hopefully. "That woman in the red hat is from Terre Haute, Indiana. Want to bet?"

Cherry, thinking at the moment about Bertha instead of watching where she was going, ran smack into a young man who was not watching where he was going, either. He was fiery-eyed, longish-haired, had spectacles with heavy black rims, and a book stuck under his nose. He muttered something, an apology, in a language Cherry had never heard before, and moved off reading. Cherry was speechless, then choked.

"Well, there's someone who isn't from Indiana. I suppose he's a poet?"

"Or a painter, or a student, or a cartoonist, or a dramatist," Gwen supplied. She added defensively, "Course, there're lots of phonies here, too. But there's an art museum down here, and a university, and fine homes, fine hotels, lots of churches—Why, even Mark Twain lived and wrote here, Miss Middle Westerner!"

While Cherry was still popeyed, Mai Lee changed the subject. "I'm starving," Mai Lee pleaded.

Cherry refused to go into an orange-painted basement eerily flickering with candlelight, insisting it looked like "a witch's cave." Gwen insisted that the place was clean and served good steaks. But Cherry said, "I'll take less romantic atmosphere—like Bertha, doggone her—and more electric lights!"

They stopped to gaze at a garden restaurant with red-and-gold lacquer balconies which trailed leaves and tinkling glass chimes. From within they heard music. The restaurant offered authentic Chinese food, prepared at your table.

"Authentic, indeed!" Mai Lee demurred. "Haven't you heard there's no chop suey in China? And no French pastry in France?"

Next they hesitated before a very pretty New England type of restaurant with maple tables and chairs, Currier and Ives prints, an inviting fire, and Yorkshire pudding and roast beef.

"Those blue walls would be the right color for the furniture. Wouldn't it, Cherry?"

"Bertha would like this place," Josie said mournfully.

Vivian pointed out that this restaurant was no novelty for any of them. "We'll take refuge here when we can't digest any more Basque or Armenian or Creole cooking."

Finally they went to the Jumble Shop, a many-roomed restaurant in an old, red stone house. Here the walls were hung with paintings by Village residents. They ate well, thinking guiltily of Bertha.

They strolled home along the foot of Fifth Avenue, pausing to look at the great, white, sculptured arch framing the entrance to Washington Square Park.

Something crossed Cherry's line of vision. It was a man in a silk hat and a woman in ermine, merrily driving along in a foreign car about the size of a matchbox.

On the walk back to the apartment, they met an East Indian woman swathed from head to foot in pale yellow veils. They bumped into a man tootling an enormous French horn as he strolled along. They dodged three excited people arguing and gesticulating in Spanish.

By now, Cherry did not even bat an eyelash.

"That's funny," Vivian said, as they turned into their own quiet side street and approached No. 9. All the lights in their apartment seemed to be out. "I left a light in the living room."

"Maybe Bertha has gone to bed."

"Or left us for good."

They groped their way into the darkened apartment, feeling more apprehensive than they cared to admit. It was a relief to see a crack of light from the back sitting room. Its door was closed. Cherry cautiously opened it, and groaned at what she saw and smelled. The other girls, sniffing, pressed forward.

"Bertha Larsen! Have you lost your mind?"

"I have made up my mind," Bertha said stubbornly, not even turning.

A bucket of bright blue paint stood on the floor. On the table, on each wooden chair, on the rickety sideboard, Bertha had thoughtfully daubed at least one blob of blue—"So that we're in for it," Cherry sighed, "and can't back out." The windows on the garden were masked with newspapers, so the janitor could not see in. It was stifling in here, without air and with the heady smell of paint. Bertha wore a small, grimly satisfied smile.

"All right, be angry with me," the big girl said. Her voice was suspiciously shaky. "But I could not look at this dirty furniture one minute longer. I *had* to put clean paint on it." She gave the table a determined lick with her dripping paintbrush. "I had to *do* something!"

The other five stared at her and at the furniture with horror-stricken faces.

"But when did you get the paint?"

"This afternoon, while the rest of you were moving furniture."

"And this is why you wouldn't come out to dinner!"

"Nor let me stay here with you," Gwen said, very subdued.

"Yes." Bertha unhappily stirred the paint. "I know, you are afraid the janitor will be angry. Well, Cherry can explain to him."

"Why me?" Cherry wailed. "*I* didn't go ahead and paint without permission. Oh, golly, we may have to pay for the furniture or get sued or some thing!"

"Well, it was your idea, Cherry," Bertha Larsen said, stubborn again.

There were frightened murmurs of "Yes, it was Cherry's idea" from the other girls. The irritated gaze which they had turned on Gwen, earlier that day, now was transferred to Cherry.

Cherry swallowed hard. She knew the girls would stand by her, but being ringleader in a situation like this was uncomfortable. Cherry could not even feel angry with Bertha: poor Bertha was so unhappy in this place that she had simply lost her head, rolled up her sleeves, and "done something."

"Well," said Cherry. "Well." She ran her hand through her curly hair. "So I have to square us with the janitor."

"Yes!" they chorused, even Gwen.

Cherry looked the Spencer Club firmly in the eye.

"All right, I will. Who's scared? Pooh. I did think up this disaster. I'll think up some way out, too."

It was sheer bravado. Cherry had not the slightest idea what she was going to do. "But I'm certainly not going to let this turn into a crisis," she thought. Everyone was tired and homesick, Bertha was still a little angry, the apartment was a shambles, the beds were not made yet—"Somebody's got to 'do something,' as Bertha says. And it looks like I'm elected."

"Huh?" said Gwen. "What are you muttering about?"

"Just this." Cherry grinned cheerfully and announced, "Here's a plan of action, kids. At least the janitor doesn't know yet. I guess he won't pop up through that trap door again. We have a little time to think. And point two, maybe Bertha was right. Anyhow, the die is cast. We can't *un*paint the furniture. So let's spend the week end painting the horrible old stuff!"

There were halfhearted but relieved murmurs of assent. Bertha put down her paintbrush and smothered Cherry in a large embrace. Gwen gave Cherry a rueful look and suggested painting the janitor blue, too.

Saturday and Sunday they painted. There was nothing else to do. Cherry kept up a cheerful front, and everyone almost had fun painting—except Cherry. For how she was going to get out of this fix, she only wished she knew. Every time she looked at her blue-stained hands, she shuddered.

"Oh, well. I have a talent for trouble. But I have a talent for wiggling out of it, too!"

CHAPTER III

The Visiting Nurses

BRIGHT AND EARLY MONDAY MORNING, THE SPENCER Club trooped out of No. 9 to report for new careers. The September air was crisp, and the city moved at a brisk pace. The girls marched along in their blue uniforms, sputtering with anticipation.

On Friday they had reported to headquarters of the Visiting Nurse Service on Murray Hill, had their applications checked over a final time, and been advised where to buy their uniforms. These were navy blue, well tailored and worn with a little white piqué bow and a navy felt roller hat.

Cherry liked the uniform for its crisp good looks, and respected it for the humane work it symbolized. She, and all the girls, wore their navy blue proudly. Their hands were a little blue too, from paint.

This morning they headed back to Madison Avenue headquarters for the first training lectures. New York roared and glistened all around them. As they mounted the steps of the stately white stone house, Vivian confided:

"Wish we were going sight-seeing this morning, instead of working!"

"Never mind," Cherry promised her. "Once we get under way on our jobs, we'll do New York. Thoroughly."

Gwen held open the black iron grille door. "We'll see New York thoroughly *on* our jobs, too. Come on!"

Bertha, Josie, and Mai Lee, bringing up the rear, were too excited to talk. All of them in their brand-new blue uniforms stared at the visiting nurses busily coming and going through these offices and halls. These young women—and many mature women, too—had a special look in their faces. It struck Cherry at once. It was as if all the suffering they had looked upon, and all the help they had given, had called forth that compassion in their eyes.

"Are you new nurses?" a woman in a suit said to them. "Report to the auditorium, please."

They found the auditorium and took seats in a row. The big room was crowded with other young women in the same blue uniform. All of them seemed grave, realizing what they were undertaking.

An older woman mounted the platform. Instantly the room became silent and attentive.

"Good morning!" She smiled at them and put her hands in her jacket pockets. "I am Mrs. Clark. Before I begin our lecture, let me congratulate you young women on becoming visiting nurses. There is no finer work—and you are urgently needed.

"I suppose you know what a visiting nurse is and does. She's the young woman in blue you'll meet hurrying over a country road in her little car to care for a sick farm child. Or you'll find her down at the water front nursing a stricken barge captain. She's the nurse who's welcomed with a sigh of relief by a sick mother and five small, bewildered children."

Mrs. Clark said this was a branch of public health nursing. Girls who entered this field must like people, for visiting nurses treated everyone who needed them, regardless of race, creed, color, or ability to pay.

"No call for help goes unanswered. None has or ever will. Last year our New York service gave nursing care to nearly *five million* sick people!"

Impressed, Cherry and her friends exchanged glances. Mrs. Clark explained that the service was paid for by the contributions of public-spirited citizens.

"You will find yourself," Mrs. Clark said, "being much more than a nurse. You will be friend and sometimes social worker, as well. Most important, you will be a teacher, instructing people in good health practices, nutrition, child care, and general hygiene. Try," she urged them, "to prevent sickness as well as to cure it. Try to help people improve their everyday living conditions."

Mrs. Clark made it dramatically clear how well this work paid off. In 1900, a child born in New York could expect to live only about thirty-four years. Now the normal life expectancy was well over sixty. Besides, the yearly death rate had been cut in half!

"Visiting nurses," Cherry thought, her eyes bright, "bring the gift of life."

Mrs. Clark told the nurses that each one would have her own district, eventually, and would answer calls for help in her own area. The service was divided into some fifteen centers, which were then subdivided into the nurses' districts. The service cooperated with doctors, hospitals, clinics, social service agencies, settlement houses, the Department of Health. It ran mothers' clubs for the instruction of expectant mothers. It provided nursing service in more than thirty day nurseries for preschool children of women who must work. It went into factories and met industrial accidents. It helped keep a vast population healthy.

"Golly," Cherry breathed. "There's more to this than taking temperatures!"

"You'll help check epidemics," Mrs. Clark told the listening young women. "You'll teach new mothers how to keep the youngest generation healthy. You'll watch out for solitary, aged people and chronic invalids who have no one to turn to except the visiting nurse.

"If your patients can pay the charge of a dollar and seventy-five cents for your three-quarter hour visit, well and good. Fifty per cent cannot afford to pay anything. But you'll find people, who can't really afford to, pressing on you fifty cents or a quarter or even five cents—out of sheer gratitude."

After lunch, Mrs. Clark announced, she would show the girls exactly how they would work.

Cherry rose and followed the Spencer Club out of the auditorium. A faint fleck of blue paint on a fingernail reminded her sharply of her predicament with the janitor. She sighed and tried to concentrate on the problem.

"What are you daydreaming about?" they innocently asked her.

"Oh, nothing," Cherry said a little bitterly. No one had been worrying much about the awful janitor since she had made her reassuring speech. No one except her. "Guess I convinced them too well, darn it."

They went down the steps of the white house into the brilliant sunshine of noon. Madison Avenue was thronged with people pouring out of skyscrapers, going to lunch. Off the six girls went, in search of restaurants.

The near-by restaurants seemed elaborate, crowded, and alarmingly expensive, at least on the salary of a beginning visiting nurse. They found a glorified sweet shop and went in. Heads turned to look at their blue uniforms.

"We're conspicuous." Vivian squirmed, as they were shown to a table.

"They're looking at Bertha's blue hair," Cherry said pointedly. The others giggled happily.

The New Yorkers, after one summarizing glance at them, quietly looked away again. "In a city as big as this," Cherry guessed, "people *have* to mind their own business or they'd be falling all over one another—by the millions!"

"I want people to notice me." Gwen sat down and tossed her red head. "I'm mighty proud of this uniform."

"I feel official," Josie Franklin stated. "Do I look official? Just think, kids, we nurses can go anywhere, practically, and do anything, almost, and—and not get murdered."

They laughed. Bertha, who had recovered her motherly and serene air, said, "Who would murder you, Josie?"

"Well, we're going into the slums, aren't we?"

The others hooted at her. "Poor doesn't mean bad. Wait and you'll see."

"No gangsters?" Josie looked disappointed.

"Here, Miss Franklin." Cherry thrust a menu card into Josie's hands. "You're apparently weak-headed from hunger."

Mai Lee sat very quiet, far off in her thoughts. The others prodded her and she sighed. "It's just that this work is going to be wonderful."

"It's the kind of nursing every nurse dreams of doing," Cherry summed it up happily.

They had some debate about what to order. There was a nice choice of sandwiches and hot dishes, but the dessert list was positively dazzling. Waitresses carried ice cream confections that made staple foods seem pointless. Cherry joked that there was as much nourishment in sugar and cream as in prosaic bread and potatoes.

"I'm going to have a dessert luncheon," she announced. "Lemon meringue pie, whipped cream apple betty, and a chocolate soda. Boy! I've always wanted to do this!"

"You can't!" said too-plump Bertha wistfully.

But they all did, Bertha included.

Back to headquarters and the auditorium they went once more. Now there was a black leather kit on the table on the platform, rather like a doctor's bag.

Mrs. Clark picked up the bag and, article by article, showed them the contents. Cherry was amazed to see how much emerged from that one compact bag.

On top lay an apron and a bundle of paper napkins. Then Mrs. Clark took out baby scales, glassware for treatments, a hypodermic set, forceps, scissors, rubber tubing, masks, cord, dressings and ties, syringe, tongue depressors, applicators, an enamel basin for sterilizing, an enamel cup, cotton, vaseline, thermometer. Out of the very bottom of the bag came record forms, soap solutions, a towel, and hand lotion for the nurse's use.

Gwen hissed, "That bag's a miniature hospital!"

"Always," Mrs. Clark was saying, "take the articles out, and return them, in exactly the same order. It will save you hunting for things." Cherry foresaw bag practice, at home.

Vivian was worried. "That bag looks awfully heavy."

It weighed only seven and a half pounds, Mrs. Clark said. She slung it comfortably on her shoulder by its long strap. Like the blue uniform, that bag was the badge of the visiting nurse. It assured her safe entry anywhere. Josie audibly sniffed.

"The first thing to do when you go into a home," Mrs. Clark said, "is to ask for a stack of newspapers. Poor families haven't many household goods, or sickroom equipment. But you can use newspapers to make substitutes. Use them as a table cover before setting down your bag. Be very, very careful not to carry infection from one home to another!"

Cherry began to imagine herself going on her first visit. What sort of home would it be? Mrs. Clark's cool voice went on:

"Take off your hat and coat and explain to the family right away about the nursing service we give. Then see the patient. Wash your hands before you take out your equipment. Of course you'll wash your hands again and sterilize your equipment in boiling water before returning it to the bag."

Josie wiggled and Gwen blew out an impatient breath. All this was familiar basic hygiene to the nurses.

"Now then! As you examine and treat the sick person, teach the rest of the family—a little at a time. Show them how to take care of the patient until you come back again. Show them how to prepare for your next visit, by getting newspapers, clearing the kitchen table, arranging a tray for the bedside treatment. Teaching is as big a part of your job as nursing. Remember that."

Mrs. Clark went into detail. Cherry, with the others, felt overwhelmed by this big helping of new information.

The visiting nurse would keep records of the patient and also of every other member of the family. She would help with all their problems, physical, emotional, or financial. Where she found a family in serious difficulties of any sort, the nurse would report it to her supervisor at the center, so that a welfare agency might be called in to assist.

"This certainly makes me feel responsible!" Cherry thought. She noticed that the entire Spencer Club was sitting up straighter.

Then there was a surge of excitement. Mrs. Clark said each nurse would now receive an envelope listing the district and center she was assigned to. Would they please stand in line?

Now with sealed envelopes in their hands, the Spencer Club disengaged itself from the other blue-clad nurses. They tumbled out of the building and, unable to wait, opened their envelopes right there on the sidewalk.

"I'm going to Long Island!" Vivian cried. "Good! It's quiet and pretty out there."

"Chinatown," read Mai Lee. "I knew it, I knew it!"

"Where's Bathgate Avenue?" Josie Franklin asked.

"Mine says Chelsea Street, wherever that is," Gwen puzzled.

Cherry looked blankly at her slip of paper and then at Bertha Larsen's. The addresses meant nothing at all to them. But Bertha, Josie, Gwen, and Cherry were all assigned to the same center!

"I knew I was lugging this thing around for some reason," Gwen muttered. She pulled forth a paper-backed guide book, and unfurled a map.

With the five-o'clock crowds swirling around them, the girls looked up their district streets. They found two Chelsea Streets, one Chelsea Square, and three Bathgate Avenues—all in widely separated parts of the five-island, five-borough city. "Not to mention all the *little* islands," Josie said helpfully. They decided simply to go home.

Home meant just one thing to Cherry. She had a sudden image of newspapers with large headlines: VANDAL NURSES PAINT, EVICTED, FINED, IMPRISONED.

"Maybe we can finish the painting, if we hurry," Mai Lee said eagerly.

"Our blue room! It's going to look well. What's the matter, Cherry? Don't you want to paint?"

"Oh, sure," said Cherry. "I'd adore to paint. But next time Ames has an idea, please ignore it."

CHAPTER IV

Ann to the Rescue

A DOUBTFUL MOOD HIT THE SPENCER CLUB OVER THE following week end. Inspiration and new work were fine but, to their disappointment, they had not been permitted to work wonders immediately. First they had to sit through more training lectures. Then had come the dampening news that they would not report to their centers until Monday.

Besides, there was still the ferocious janitor to deal with. Although this problem was labeled "Cherry's responsibility," the Spencer Club was completing the painting with diminished blitheness. Every time they passed the trap door, even though it was firmly nailed down, they looked apprehensive. When the doorbell rang this rainy Saturday morning, they jumped.

"You go, Cherry."

"You're nearer the door, Bertha. You go."

"Gwen is nearer than I am." Gwen made a face at Bertha and did not budge.

The doorbell shrilled again. Josie timidly went over and opened it a crack. A lady in draperies and a man with a harp stood there. The girls stared, goggle-eyed. In fine, ringing diction, the woman enunciated:

"Is this by any chance the Garibaldi Music and Debating Society?"

"No'm, by no chance," Josie stuttered and closed the door by falling on it.

They all let out sighs of relief.

"I think," said Cherry, winding one black curl around her finger, "that we ought to get out of here today. Go sight-seeing or something. Anything to dodge the janitor a while longer."

"Sight-seeing in the rain?" Bertha said sensibly.

"We won't melt. Honestly, if that doorbell rings again, I'll have nervous prostration."

"We'll all collapse with you," Gwen sympathized.

The doorbell rang again. The four girls sat frozen. In a whisper Gwen said:

"There's no law that says we *have* to answer the doorbell."

Cherry hissed back, "I'll die of curiosity if we don't."

Like a man going to his doom, Cherry plodded to the door and opened it. It was not the janitor. It was a pleasant, well-dressed woman who smiled and said:

"I'm your neighbor, Mrs. Jenkins. My husband and I live directly above you. I just stopped in to say that if you ever need help, Mr. Jenkins and I are within call."

"How kind of you!" Cherry exclaimed. "That's good to know. Won't you come in, Mrs. Jenkins?"

Their neighbor shook her head. "I'm too busy just now, thanks. But I thought you all looked rather homesick. Would this help?" She held out a basket of steaming hot gingerbread.

"Oh, thank you, thank you!" the girls exclaimed. As the neighbor smiled and vanished up the stairs, they decided New Yorkers were not so bad, after all.

When the doorbell rang a third time, Cherry paled. Not one of the girls stirred. Cherry whispered, "Our luck couldn't hold out three times in a row!" They waited, without moving a muscle, while the doorbell rang furiously again and then they heard footsteps clumping away. A second later, outside their windows, they saw the top of the janitor's head.

"There, I told you!" Cherry gasped. "He knows we're home and he's on our trail. We absolutely must get out of here!"

The girls ruefully agreed. They decided to wake Vivian and Mai Lee, who were busy sleeping till noon. At least, they were asleep until a kitchen shelf collapsed, raining pots and pans. A second later, the usual three fire engines went shrieking past their windows. The sleepers awoke with shouts of protest.

The telephone rang. Cherry seized it. "Oh frabjous day!"

"Hello, what's the matter?" said Ann Evans's calm, amused voice.

"Ann! Oh, how wonderful to talk to you! When are you coming down to see us?"

"Soon, if you'll have me. How are you all?" Ann's voice was so cool, so close, that Cherry could almost see her friend's steady, dark-blue eyes and feel her poised presence. But Gwen took the phone away. All the girls insisted on taking turns talking with Ann.

"Ann wants us to call her back later and make a date," Vivian said, as she hung up. "What's this mad talk about doing New York in the rain?"

Josie wailed. She had just discovered she was wearing Mai Lee's slip by mistake. "And besides, Cherry, where'll we go? We haven't much to spend."

"Yes, that's right!"

Cherry bit her lip. "Uh—ah—we'll go to"—she said the first thing that popped into her head—"the Statue of Liberty."

They looked interested despite themselves. But then Vivian and Mai Lee wanted to stay home and sleep.

"And face the janitor all by yourselves?" Cherry warned.

They glared at Cherry with her flushed cheeks and bobbing black curls.

"Doggone you, Cherry Ames," Gwen said, slowly getting out of her chair, "why do you have to be a self-starter?" The others rose too.

The trek to the Statue of Liberty was not an unqualified success, but it kept them out of the janitor's clutches. To get to the Battery, they fumbled around in roaring subways and emerged, thoroughly bewildered, at the foot of Wall Street skyscrapers. Here they found a tremendous stretch of grass, Bowling Green, and New York harbor. Gray ships steamed out of sight on a gray ocean.

Almost no one was out in the rain this Saturday except the six girls, pigeons, and a peanut vendor under a huge, dripping umbrella. They bought bags of peanuts and caught the ridiculous little boat going over to Bedloe Island, on which the statue stood. The boat's other passengers were a group of visiting Texans, shivering but conscientious, and a knot of young sailors going sailing for a holiday, and—Cherry was informed by three small boys who shared her peanuts—the Wild Eagle Boy Scout Troop.

"It's better than the janitor, anyhow," Cherry thought.

They sailed out in the rain and the statue loomed up gray and enormous. Dashing from the boat up to the statue's base, they felt like pygmies. Then they were inside the hollow, metal statue. It was electrically lighted and winding straight up it were spiral stairs, iron and exceedingly steep and narrow.

They started climbing and in no time at all they were puffing. Cherry began to feel muscles pulling in her legs that she had forgotten she possessed. Bertha Larsen's hat tipped to one side of her head. Up and round, up and round they climbed. "*You* thought this up!" the girls hissed at Cherry. "You thought up painting the furniture, too!" But when they reached the top, the Spencer Club voted it worth the effort.

They were standing in the statue's forehead. Under the rays of her crown were windows. The girls could see all of New York harbor and its skyline, and the Atlantic stretching away to the Old World. Cherry hung out one of the windows and, by painfully twisting her neck, contrived to look up. Above her soared the statue's smooth, mammoth arm, upraised, the hand grasping the torch of freedom. Cherry's neck was stiff for an hour afterward, but she would never forget the solemn thrill that went through her at that moment.

"The statue needs a paint job," Bertha commented.

They all turned on her. "Will you shush!"

The descent down the steep spiral was even more dizzying than the climb up. "At least the janitor won't look for us here," Gwen cheered them on. No one tripped, however, and they ended up lunching belatedly at the hot dog concession outside in the rain.

"Let's go shopping," Vivian suggested. "Mm, pretty clothes!" Her soft eyes sparkled.

They plodded up to midtown via boat, subway, and Fifth Avenue bus. They were six dripping and bedraggled nurses who entered the gleaming doors of Saks Fifth Avenue.

In spite of the rain, the store was crowded. Cherry was so taken by the beautiful things on display that she almost forgot her "responsibility." What dazzled her even more were these women shoppers, beautifully dressed, perfectly groomed.

"They look like they're going to a party!" Bertha Larsen marveled. "Will you look at their hairdos!"

"Look!" squeaked Josie. "Not one of them's wearing rubbers!"

"Their furs, oh, their luscious hats," moaned Vivian. "And their jewelry!"

Gwen was at a counter, happily burrowing into a heap of bright silk scarfs. As the other five came up to drag her forth, they caught sight of themselves in a large mirror. Simultaneously they halted. Against a background of fashion-plate women stood five soaking, smudge-faced girls, with wisps of hair sticking every which way, and horrified eyes.

"Oh, shame, is that us?"

"I distinctly see that saleswoman sniffing at us!"

"Let's get out of here!"

All six of them turned tail and fled. They rode home under the beaten title of The Ragpickers.

At their apartment, they felt reasonably safe, for it was late. Late enough for the janitor not to bother them any more today. Mail was waiting for them.

The girls turned on lights and scattered, curling up in various rooms to read their letters. Cherry had just picked up hers when the doorbell rang. Without thinking, she answered it.

It was the janitor.

"So ye been dodgin' me all day!" he growled at Cherry. "Lemme in!"

The other girls came running and stared, crestfallen, at the gnarled little man.

"No, no, you can't come in!" Cherry stuttered. "You can't!"

"I got a perfect right to come in. Got to see that trap door, I ain't satisfied with it. Now lemme in!"

The girls crowded to the door in an unconscious surge, barring his way.

"Lemme in!" he roared. "Want me to report ye to the landlord?"

Cherry visibly shook. The janitor pushed his way into their living room. All eyes turned to Cherry, mutely signaling, "This is *your* responsibility, remember?" Cherry swallowed a large lump in her throat.

"Mr.—uh—Mr.—couldn't you come back next week?"

"Naw, I couldn't. The name is Sam. Out o' my way."

He strode down the hall, hammer and screw drivers clanking. The trap door was back there. Only a little farther on was the back parlor with its freshly painted furniture. The door was open, the lights were on. If the janitor did not happen to see the blue furniture, the smell of paint would surely lead him in there.

"Oh, why was I born?" Cherry moaned.

Fingers pressed into her sides and back. "Follow him!" the girls hissed. "Do something!"

"Yes, talk him out of it!"

The girls forcibly pushed Cherry forward.

"Remember, you thought this up," Bertha intoned.

At that moment the janitor turned around. They all held their breaths.

"And furthermore!" he growled. "About the garbage!"

Cherry's voice trembled. "What about the garbage?"

"Ye can't just throw 'er out. Oh, no! It hasta be wrapped just so. In newspaper. Tied. The landlord says so. He's very partic'lar. Very."

Gwen said tartly, "Is the landlord as bad as you?" Instantly the other girls made motions of distress and faces meaning: "Be quiet! What are you trying to do?"

The janitor glared. "Look, Miss Smarty. If ye really want to know, I have a key to your place and I could come in any time I want to. But I've been polite about it, see? I ain't a tyrant because I like it. I got my orders. The landlord is a hard man. If ye think I'm tough, ye should meet up with him sometime. I only wish it to ye."

Cherry abruptly sat down. "This is just dandy," she murmured. But the other girls lifted her to her feet and shoved her forward again.

"Paint!" The janitor let out a yelp. "Do I smell paint? Hey! What's goin' on here?"

He looked to Cherry like a knotted, evil gnome as he stamped into the back parlor. Surveying the furniture, his back stiffened and he let out another yell.

"Now ye've done it! Ye'll have to buy a new dining-room set for sure! Ye'll be lucky if the landlord don't evict ye, besides!"

Hands pushed Cherry down the hall. She turned around once to mumble and implore, but it did no good.

"Sam—" she quavered. "Sam, listen—"

"Didn't I tell ye not to paint without permission of me? Didn't I warn ye? Just wait till the landlord finds out! Oh, I pity ye, ye poor idiots! I wouldn't want to face the landlord in your shoes! When he sees how ye broke the rules and defaced his property—"

"We'll pay," Cherry choked out, "we'll make it good—"

"Ye got paint on the floor, besides! Not only ruinin' the furniture, ye injured the building! Vandals!"

"Sam, please, don't tell the landlord yet—"

"Ye might as well pack up. Ever see eviction papers? Or court orders for a big, fat bill? Ye'll see 'em now!"

The janitor knelt beside the trap door and started hammering with a vengeance. Each furious blow might have been meant for these undesirable tenants. Over the noise Cherry pleaded in vain. Sam shook his head and finally stalked out.

"Ye'll be hearin' from the landlord," he threw over his shoulder.

In the terrible silence that followed, Josie spoke up: "Well. Guess I'll read my letters now. Cherry promised to get us out of this, and I guess she will, all right."

The other girls, with black looks, retired amid mutters of "Eviction!" "Two or three hundred dollars for new furniture for the landlord!"

Cherry took a sharp hold on her emotions and, with a wrench of will power, calmed down. She paced around the apartment, thinking. That awful janitor was not joking. The possibility of having to pay for the furniture, or even of being asked to move, was very real.

Suddenly she stood still and exclaimed: "Now why didn't I think of that before!"

"Are you still thinking up things?" Gwen asked wearily. Her freckled face changed to alarm as Cherry snatched up her coat. "What are you up to now?"

"Just a slight errand. Be right back." She wanted to keep this secret, in case the answer was no.

Cherry hastened out the front door and onto the street. The rain had ceased, the moon shone down on city chimneys, and she heard singing and the rumble of the subway underground. She felt relieved already.

In a drugstore phone booth, she dialed Ann.

"Ann, it's me. You've been living in New York long enough to know the worst about janitors and landlords, haven't you?—Well, Jack has, hasn't he?—Maybe the two of you can help, because—"

Ann's chuckles punctuated Cherry's earnest narrative.

"All right," Ann replied. "I'll be down tomorrow afternoon. In the meantime, give me your landlord's name and address—what? Spell it.—All right, Jack and I will see what we can do. 'Bye."

Cherry almost skipped home. Ann and Jack might not be able to do anything except advise her. Still, even that would be a help. She could wait for tomorrow and Ann with an easier mind.

Now Cherry pounced on her letters and settled down to read them. She opened the one from her mother first. Even the familiar handwriting and Hilton postmark were enough to chase away worries.

"It's unusually and wonderfully peaceful around our house now," Mrs. Ames wrote. "With you away and Charles off to the university and Midge back in high school (thank goodness), I am at last getting the fall house cleaning accomplished. Velva—remember her?—is helping me. Dad complains that he gets chased from room to room. But the house will look nice when you come home for visits. I am sending you some more stockings, a chocolate mahogany cake, and Dad insists on putting this in, too." "This" was a check. "He says it's for a treat for the Spencer Club. Much love from us both—Mother."

Cherry ran around the apartment waving the check. "Hey! My dad is treating us!"

"How very nice of him!"

"Wonderful. To what?"

"To anything we want, I guess," Cherry said.

"Curtains!" they chorused. Mai Lee said, "We feel like we're residing in a goldfish bowl."

Cherry, much cheered by her letter from home, galloped back to read the rest of her letters. There was a note from Midge reporting that she was really looking out for her father, and Dr. Joe was looking better as a result. Charlie wrote that he was terrifically busy with his engineering courses, liked them fine, and had found many old friends on campus.

"Best for the last," Cherry murmured, and turned to the letter from Wade Cooper. The tall, brown-eyed, brown-skinned flier had been her pilot when Cherry was a flight nurse, serving overseas. Now he was back in Tucson, his home town, grounded with an auto repair business.

"If I don't see you soon, Cherry," Wade wrote, "I am going to burst. You wouldn't want that to happen, would you? Think I'll come to New York and pay you a visit. That is, as soon as this danged business will pay my fare."

So Wade would be coming to New York! Hurray! When Cherry told the other nurses Wade was coming and had sent his regards to them, they all were pleased.

"Supper!" called Bertha, interrupting the discussion. The Spencer Club adjourned to supper and, not long afterward, to bed.

Next day, Sunday, the members of the Spencer Club were quiet as mice, to discourage the janitor, in case he had any ideas. The sun shone, and peace descended on the Village. The girls practiced bag technique in the morning, rather guilty at having put it off so long. Then they answered their letters. Josie, as the club's corresponding secretary, importantly wrote a report to Marie Swift. For a long time the only sounds in the apartment were pens scratching on paper.

Cherry made it a point to write to Dr. Joe. "The visiting nurse service puts discoveries like yours, Dr. Joe," she wrote, "into widespread, everyday use." She knew he would be interested.

Cherry also wrote to Wade Cooper, notifying him that New York, the Spencer alumni, and particularly herself, would be delighted to see him any time he could come.

That afternoon the doorbell emitted three short rings. It was Ann's signal. The girls let her in with greetings of pleasure and relief.

"Why are you smuggling me in like this?" Ann laughed. "Now, wait—I didn't guarantee to work miracles! Can't we have a visit first?"

Ann Evans, now Mrs. Jack Powell, was the same calm Ann with whom they had gone through nurses' training. Her dark-blue eyes were still as steady as Cherry remembered them. Her smooth, brown hair was arranged a new way and she wore a blue dress which Cherry had never seen before—otherwise Ann looked exactly the same.

"Marriage hasn't changed you a bit, Mrs. Powell!" Cherry teased, after greeting her.

"Why should it?" Ann smiled. "I gather Jack married me because he liked me more or less the way I was."

"But—but—" Josie blurted, "I thought you'd at least get a different expression, or *something*!"

Ann shook her head and murmured that none of them had changed noticeably, either. Cherry saw her glance with some concern at too-thin Vivian. "Your apartment looks nice," Ann said. "I came down to help. Give me an apron and a chore."

"We're not going to do another thing to the apartment until the janitor decides our fates," Cherry told her. "He's a gnome, an ogre, a—a—" she broke off and gave Ann a sly look. "Or do you have a plan of action, Ann?"

"I have." Ann's eyes danced.

"Ann!" the others chorused. "Did Cherry tell you? Are you going to help her get us out of this scrape?"

But Ann only said, "I do think you might inquire after my husband."

"How's Jack?" they asked, ashamedly.

"He's very well. I'll tell you my plan presently. Now can't we have a visit?"

Under Ann's quieting influence, they settled down for a long talk. With her they exchanged news, stopped to quibble, laughed at Ann's accounts of housekeeping. Cherry was doubly glad to see her old friend and classmate, for Ann came from Indian City, near Hilton, and knew Charlie. The afternoon wore on. They talked and talked, and it was evening before they knew it.

"Won't you tell us the plan now? Please!"

"I was going to invite you all for Sunday night supper." Ann's dark-blue eyes twinkled at them. "But Jack's parents are visiting us and—while they're darlings—I was afraid two elderly people and you imps might not combine. So I trust you'll permit me to have supper with you."

"Shall we let her stay?"

"Well, just this once. As a special concession."

"Oh, thank you, thank you! As a token of my gratitude, I will introduce you to"—Ann paused for dramatic effect—"your landlord."

There was a puzzled pause. Gwen said glumly, "I know him already."

"You saw him just once, when you signed the lease. Is that it? Well," Ann had a wise air, "you are now going to meet him informally. As a friend."

"Oh!" said Cherry, beginning to understand. "But will you please stop impersonating the Sphinx?"

"Get your coats," said Ann, blandly grinning. "We are going to an Italian restaurant where your landlord, for old times' sake, has his Sunday evening supper."

The girls went for their hats and coats.

Strolling south of Bleecker Street and leaving Greenwich Village behind, Ann explained. In her husband's office worked a young man of Italian descent, whose uncle was in the real estate business, who had a friend, who was the Spencer Club's landlord.

"Simple," Ann said, still grinning. "Your Mr. Ramiglia knows we're coming. Dickie—in Jack's office—fixed it for you. We'll have supper in that restaurant, too. I've been there once, Dickie took us. For practically no money, you get heaps of the most wonderful food. I think I could look at that menu again and pick out something besides the date."

"You mean the menu is in Italian?"

"I have plenty of misgivings about the landlord!"

"Since when do you speak Italian, Ann?"

"She doesn't."

"Neither do any of us."

"We'll starve in that restaurant!"

"Never mind a little thing like starving. Think of facing the landlord!"

Ann remained unruffled. They had entered a neighborhood where many Italian-American families lived. It was like any other part of town, except for the Roman-sounding names on the shopwindows and a few unusual wares. The people looked like the rest of town, except for their liquid, dark eyes and an extra vivacity. Here and there was a gesturing grandmother with a shawl over her head, or an old man in a rakish black hat reading an Italian-language newspaper. But anyone under fifty was thoroughly American, the younger the more so, right down to the angelic-faced children busy reading the Sunday funny papers.

"The place we're going to is called the Grand Paradiso," Ann said, leading the way. "20 1/2 Derby Street."

"Can't be very grand if it's only a half," Gwen ribbed her.

"Wait till you meet Mama and Papa Mediterraneo. Wait till you taste Mama's *pasta*."

"Wait till we meet the landlord!"

"Thank goodness, that's Cherry's responsibility. Stop groaning, Cherry."

The restaurant was a small store with a few white-clothed tables and a kitchen at the back. Papa Mediterraneo, the waiter and cashier, was quite an old man.

He remembered Ann, and bowing and smiling led the girls to a table. The landlord was nowhere in sight.

Mama Mediterraneo, a monumental old lady with satiny, coal-black hair, in a spick-and-span gingham dress, came out of her kitchen to beam at them. Diamonds flashed in her ears, and her eyes and teeth flashed nearly as brilliantly. Cherry did not understand the voluble Italian but the tone of voice was unmistakable. She smiled back and that was enough. The Mediterraneos, laughing at the girls, took away the menus. They gestured that Mama would outdo herself for Signora Powell and her friends.

And then Mr. Ramiglia came out of the kitchen, beaming and carrying a platter of ravioli. Two small boys tagged at his heels, bearing plates and silverware.

"Hello, Mrs. Powell," Mr. Ramiglia said, coming over to their table. He was a stocky, middle-aged, fatherly looking man. "These are my sons, Johnny and Joe. Are these your frightened young ladies?" He looked amused. "Oh, yes, Miss Jones. I remember you. How are you?"

Gwen looked uncertain as to whether she wished to be remembered or not. She stuck a blue-stained hand in her pocket.

"Mr. Ramiglia, my friends mistakenly—" Ann started.

"Mr. Ramiglia, we painted the—" Cherry gulped.

"You mean you painted that dining-room set?" He waved a hand, gave a forkful of ravioli to Johnny, then one to Joe. "That old, dilapidated set? Fine, fine."

"Then you don't mind—" Bertha said slowly.

"I hope you didn't spend too much on the paint. Furniture isn't worth it." He set the platter down on the table next to theirs, seated himself, and took a big mouthful of ravioli. "Order ravioli. Take my advice. Come, boys, sit down."

Cherry turned full around in her chair, eyes like saucers. "But, Mr. Ramiglia! Your janitor—he—"

"He scared you?"

Suddenly they all burst out laughing.

"Sam scares everybody. It is his one pleasure in life. Pay no attention. I will speak to him, maybe on the phone tonight. Johnny! Don't eat so fast. No, Joe, no—"

When Mr. Ramiglia turned back to his ravioli the girls looked deep into one another's eyes. All that worrying and tiptoeing for nothing!

"You see," said Ann softly, "even in New York landlords aren't so terrible."

Cherry felt ten years younger. Her appetite, which had lagged all week, returned to normal, particularly when a platter of ravioli arrived for them.

Never in her life had Cherry eaten such magnificent food as came out of Mama Mediterraneo's kitchen. What went into it even Bertha could not guess, beyond pure olive oil, fresh mushrooms, and the best Texas beef. Then came frozen pudding with almonds. They ate in a sort of rapture, while Papa Mediterraneo stood over them emitting cries of approval and Mr. Ramiglia smiled across the little restaurant. When Papa Mediterraneo gave them their check, it was only fifty cents apiece. They could not believe it.

"You know what?" Cherry asked, after they had exchanged cordial good-byes with the Mediterraneos and Mr. Ramiglia and staggered out into the street. "I think our landlord is a human being. I think our janitor is a character, to put it mildly. I think New Yorkers who eat any place except at the Grand Paradiso are crazy."

"They don't know about it," Ann replied.

"They should, when it's right in their own town," Cherry retorted. "It's a shame for people to keep cooking like that to themselves! Maybe it's time all the people of different antecedents got better acquainted."

Bertha nodded wisely. "Wait. I will take you to a Swedish smorgasbord restaurant my uncle's brother-in-law runs. I mean, if we can ever eat again."

Mai Lee said she was almost too full to talk, but offered, "I'll take you to Canal Street someday. We'll have Chinese roast duck."

"I mean more than restaurants," Cherry persisted. "I mean—I mean—I just have an idea."

"You told us to ignore you whenever you had one of your ideas," Bertha warned.

"But this is a good idea!"

"You mean," Vivian prodded gently, "it's a new one, so you're rarin' to go."

"No, it's a good idea."

Gwen sighed. "Well, what is it? Tell us in advance, so we'll have time to duck."

"I'm—not sure," Cherry said. "I have only a piece of an idea so far. But wait!"

When they arrived back at No. 9, a gnarled, gnomish figure was waiting on the step. It was the janitor. He approached them politely and said, in tones they had never heard issue from him before:

"Is there anything you young ladies would like? A stepladder? Or some fuses, or—or anything?"

They gasped. Cherry had just presence of mind enough left to say:

"Could you lend us an extra paintbrush?"

CHAPTER V

Tryout

THE CENTER TO WHICH CHERRY, GWEN, BERTHA AND Josie reported on Monday morning was in an obscure section of the city which they had never seen before. They hunted up the address and found a small, brick building wedged in among several larger factories and stores, on a busy, shabby street.

"Our center!" Cherry announced with a flourish. She did not feel nearly so merry and assured as she sounded. The black bag slung from her shoulder was a weight on her mind, as well.

"So this is 'home.' " Gwen scowled at the noncommittal building. "What do you suppose it's going to be like?"

"One way to find out is to go in," Bertha observed matter-of-factly.

"Wait!" Josie Franklin drew a deep breath and righted her navy blue roller. "I'm all undone from that wild subway ride!"

"Ready now? Forward! Courage!" Cherry impatiently opened the door and the other three followed her in. They found people waiting on some long benches, then a switchboard and a very busy operator. They went on in.

This was a big, plain, sunny office. At long tables fifteen or eighteen blue-clad nurses were just settling themselves with piles of documents. Two executive-looking women worked at desks. At the far end of the room, Cherry saw rows of filing cabinets, a row of typewriters, and several young women who evidently were the clerical staff.

Telephones were everywhere, ringing constantly. The only medical things Cherry saw were some examining booths—or perhaps they were used for interviews—and some bright-colored posters.

A smiling young woman approached the four new nurses. She was not much older than they were, and she had an efficient air and a twinkle in her brown eyes which reassured them. She said very rapidly:

"You must be Miss Franklin, Miss Larsen—how do you do!—Miss Jones and, er, Miss Ames. I'll have your names and faces straight in a moment! I'm Miss Davis, Dorothy Davis, your supervisor. Will you come over to my desk?"

Like a flash Miss Davis was off across the busy room. The girls sprinted after her. She already had pulled forward four chairs around her desk, and waved them into them. An athletic girl carrying an armful of folders loped up, and Miss Davis drew her forward.

"And this is Ethel Hall, your unit's clerk. Ethel—only we call her Bobbie—is general co-ordinator and trouble shooter. Just ask her for anything you need."

Ethel—or Bobbie—grinned at them. She had dancing, light-blue eyes, tennis muscles, and extreme youth. She turned to grin affectionately at the supervisor.

"I'll look out for 'em, Miss Davis." Their family report forms were ready for them, and Bobbie would show them how the Filing Department worked. "Oh, Miss Davis, Mrs. Tchechl had her baby this morning at six o'clock. Want a layette assigned? I saved one."

"Good. Yes." Miss Davis signed a requisition slip which Bobbie thrust out for her. They held a rapid-fire conversation before the four interested new arrivals.

"Where are Mr. Smith's false teeth?"

"Coming at two this afternoon."

"What word on the runaway girl?"

"Police are working on it but nothing definite yet. Do you want me to buy cakes for the Mothers' Club tea or are we broke again?"

"We're broke, all right, but three of the mothers offered to bake cakes. Tell Nurse Sullivan, doctors' conference, ten tomorrow, on her suspected smallpox carrier. She's invited. Tell Nurse Kane," said Dorothy Davis without pausing for breath, "special diet allowance approved by headquarters for the Doremus case. Tell Nurse Marrow thanks for her fountain pen and here it is."

The supervisor handed a pen to Bobbie who said, "Yes, ma'am, Miss Davis!" grinned again at the newcomers, and dashed off. Two telephones rang on Miss Davis's desk. She answered them both at once, while the four new nurses looked on in amazement. In two minutes she had arranged for a moving van and a class in child care. Cherry had seen plenty of teamwork but never as speedy and easygoing as this.

"Well, now!" said Miss Davis. She had hung up and sat back comfortably in her desk chair. "I'll introduce you to your fellow nurses in a moment. We're all really awfully glad to have you here. You certainly are needed! To start with, you'll be floaters, then you'll be assigned to your own districts. Providing, of course," Dorothy Davis said briskly, "that you make good on this job. But of course you will.

"You'll each go out in the mornings, today and tomorrow, with an experienced nurse. Additional lectures when and if Mrs. Clark specifies. Then you'll go out alone on a few selected cases. At the end of this week, I'll go out on the districts with you, to see how you're getting along, and to help you."

"We're going out *alone*? This very first week?" Josie Franklin wailed. Cherry and Gwen and Bertha looked uncertain, too.

"Why, of course! Don't be afraid to ask me questions—or to ask me for help. That's what I'm here for. Or go to Mrs. Berkey, she's assistant supervisor—introduce you in a moment."

Cherry let out her breath. Since this Davis dynamo casually expected instantaneous wonders from them, perhaps they might measure up, at that. Her confidence was catching! Miss Davis raced on to describe the daily routine.

Mornings, for an hour or two, the nurses wrote up their visits of the previous day in the folder maintained for each family. These were called case records. The nurses read and answered mail from their patients. These letters, Miss Davis said, were lively reading and she handed the four new nurses a note that had come in this morning: *"Dolling Nurs I bag you plis to com not sick nomor but nu Girl babe!! we name him four you, plis duet now Resp."*

If mail as touching as that could be called "daily routine," Cherry reflected, this job must be extraordinary!

"—then Bobbie will give you your list of calls for the day and the doctors' orders, and you'll go out on the district," Miss Davis was continuing. "If you get lost or stymied, phone back to the office. Phone back, anyhow, to see if any new calls have come in for you. You don't have to return here at five o'clock, unless you want to leave your bags or change into street clothes. Have your lunch at any restaurant you can find. You see, you'll be strictly on your own."

Cherry gulped. It sounded grueling, challenging, lonely—but an adventure in human dealings! Judging by Gwen's shining eyes and tight lips, she must be feeling the same way. Bertha and Josie looked awed.

Dorothy Davis turned a warming smile on them. "You'll come to love this work, and you'll really care about the people on your districts," she promised them. For all her dash and speed, Dorothy Davis had the graciousness which all the people in this work radiated.

Next Miss Davis introduced them to the assistant supervisor, Mrs. Berkey, a tall, capable woman whose gray eyes looked through and through the newcomers. Cherry did not find her as approachable as Miss Davis. But she liked the nurses very much. They were not only a friendly, sturdy lot, but surprisingly cheerful. Cherry was startled to hear them address one another as "Snookie" and the two supervisors as "Miss and Mrs. Snookie."

Miss Davis explained to the newcomers with a grin.

"We joke a lot in the office—to offset the grim things we see every day. If we didn't laugh, we'd cry. And we'd rather laugh."

She introduced each new nurse to the experienced nurse who was to take her in tow. Cherry was assigned to a nurse named Mary Cornish who seemed to be shy and tongue-tied. She was slight and quiet, and Cherry felt Mary Cornish should be under *her* wing, not the other way around. She watched Gwen, Josie, and Bertha each go off meekly with her nurse guide.

Cherry sat down beside Mary Cornish at one of the long tables, in the midst of the blue-clad nurses. A puddle of sunshine danced on the case folders. The nurses' chatter and laughter rippled up and down the table. Cherry felt as if she had strayed into a lively sorority, rather than an office.

"Now, Miss Ames, don't you want to look over the case records of the families we're going to visit this morning?" Mary Cornish suggested in her shy, pleasant voice. "I'll be finished here in a few minutes and then we'll leave."

One of the folders was nearly empty. Miss Cornish explained that this was a new case, and they would have to gather information about the family's members on their first visit, today. She handed Cherry family forms to put in her black bag. "You'll take the family history."

"But—but—" Cherry scowled. "Will they be willing to tell a stranger about their private lives?"

"A visiting nurse *isn't* a stranger. Never, never," said Mary Cornish with her gentle smile. Cherry resolved to watch closely how this quiet nurse worked with her families. Perhaps the right method would end her feeling of being an intruder.

They set out in the sunshine, swinging along with their bags. The city street teemed with life. Nurse Cornish said they could take a streetcar, but would have to walk so far at the other end that it was simpler to walk the whole way. She settled into a long, easy stride, and Cherry tried to imitate her.

"This is pretty hard work, isn't it, Miss Cornish?"

"Interesting work," Mary Cornish quietly corrected her. "It's—fascinating when you do it. It's hard to explain. When you go into somebody's house, for instance, and they rush to the door and say, 'Oh, thank goodness, here's the nurse'—well, that's sort of wonderful," the little nurse finished shyly. "Everybody knows our uniform."

After walking fifteen minutes and what seemed to Cherry like many miles, they came to blocks of tenements under an elevated line. Elevated trains at intervals roared past tenement windows. Poorly clad people haggled and joked at pushcarts at the curb, bearing vegetables, aprons, and shoelaces. The small shops were another meeting place. Women visited on stoops and "minded" one another's babies in peeling carriages. A singing organ-grinder and an old man shouting "I buy old clothes!" joined the cries of playing children. Dozens of people turned to say "Hello, nurse!" as Mary Cornish and Cherry threaded their way up the lively street.

"This is *my* district," Mary Cornish said. "I've been on it five years. I helped bring that little boy"—she nodded toward a handsome youngster bouncing a ball—"into the world. And see that pretty woman? Morning, Mrs. Castroviejo! She'd almost surely be blind if all the health services hadn't helped. It does me good to see her sitting there in the sun embroidering blouses. That's how she makes her living, you know. Why, Mr. Levy!" Nurse Cornish paused to wave at an old man sitting in an open window, wrapped in overcoat and blankets. "Good for you, to be up! Don't stay up too long! Pneumonia case," she explained to Cherry.

The district nurse stopped to inquire after an absent son and to pat a child on the head, then led Cherry into a narrow, shabby building.

Cherry stared around the murky hallway out of which rose steep, rickety, wooden stairs.

"Fifth floor," said Mary Cornish cheerfully. "Our patients usually live on the top floor, where it costs less." She started up.

Cherry collided in the near-dark with a baby carriage left in the hall, tripped on a cracked step, and climbed up after Miss Cornish's small figure. On the second floor, with its four apartment doors, radio music and the smell of cabbage soup greeted them. A yapping poodle met them on the third floor. On the fourth floor, Cherry had to rest, panting for breath. Mary Cornish smiled and waited, not winded a bit. On the fifth floor, a door stood ajar for them.

"At least it's sunny again, away up here," Cherry muttered.

Mary Cornish rang the doorbell and sang out, "Good morning, Mrs. Crump! It's the nurse!"

Mrs. Crump was a large, woebegone woman propped in bed, unable to stir from there. Her leg, from hip to foot, was in a plaster cast. At the sight of the nurses, she brightened.

"Thank goodness, you're here! I *told* Mr. Crump not to worry but to go off to his job. I *told* him you'd not fail me. Why, howje-do, Miss Ames, I'm glad to meet you. Glad to have visitors."

Chatting with the lonesome woman, Cherry followed Nurse Cornish's example, took off her hat, tied on her apron, and washed her hands. Newspapers were already spread on a table beside the bed. The small room was as clean and orderly as Mr. Crump, presumably, could manage.

"I broke my leg, yessiree, Miss Ames, fell down a whole flight of stairs and broke my leg," Mrs. Crump announced with evident pride. "Mrs. Remus, downstairs, she broke only her ankle. But I broke my hip too!"

Cherry smiled and helped Mary Cornish get the woman ready for a bed bath. After bathing her, the nurse checked her temperature and pulse, and made sure she had no new symptoms. They remade her bed with clean linens, then cleaned and straightened the room, and the kitchen and living room beyond. A photograph of a man with ferocious mustaches glared down at them from the wall.

"That's Mr. Crump," Mary Cornish whispered to Cherry as they dusted. "Actually he's as gentle as a lamb. Did you see the sandwiches on the bedside table? Mr. Crump fixes them every morning and cleans house a little, before he goes to his motorman's job."

"How does Mrs. Crump manage on the days you can't come?" Cherry whispered back.

"Oh, the neighbors look out for her. The woman next door brings her hot soup, and the children downstairs come up every afternoon and read aloud to her."

Back in the bedroom, Mrs. Crump seemed refreshed from her bath and begged the nurses to stay and chat. But the house cleaning—rarely done, but an emergency to be met here—had taken half an hour and other people were waiting for them. Mary Cornish tactfully explained, and added:

"But I brought you the sewing kit you've been asking for. Now you can turn the collars on your husband's shirts."

Mrs. Crump held out her large arms eagerly. "I can't tell you how it irks me to sit here doing nothing. I'm going to sew like a house afire! Thanks, nurse!"

After this case of general care, they proceeded to a building around the corner. This one was really dilapidated. As they labored up six crazy flights of steps, this time, Cherry marveled that the old staircase did not come crashing down with them.

At the top, a brood of children swirled around Nurse Cornish, whispering excitedly.

Cherry followed them into an apartment that was in pleasant contrast to the building itself. Although the rooms were tiny and crowded, the furniture drab and worn, still this was home. Everything was immaculate and in order. Homemade toys were stacked in a corner, a stew bubbled fragrantly on the stove, and starched if threadbare curtains hung at all the shining-clean windows.

The children, too, were threadbare but scrubbed. They ranged in age from Tommy, who was seven (he was not in school this morning because of his cold), through Jenny, four, the twins Molly and Mark, who were two and a half, down to the baby asleep in its crib. They reported wide-eyed that their father and two sisters—"big girls, ten 'n' 'leven"—had risen at five in this emergency to do the day's chores, then left the sick mother "in our care!"

They were well-behaved, self-reliant children. Tommy pretended valiantly, "for the little kids," not to be frightened at seeing their mother lying helpless. Cherry felt sorry for these bewildered little folk.

She felt even sorrier when she saw the wan, hollow-eyed woman who lay exhausted and very ill in the stuffy bedroom. Nurse Cornish sent the children into another room on invented errands, while she quickly examined the woman. Cherry handed her the doctor's instructions for this pneumonia patient, and hastily went through the usual routine until her bag's contents were spread on a newspaper-covered table. Then she hurried into the kitchen to boil some water.

The children tagged at Cherry's heels. "Will our mama get well?"

"Of course she will!" Cherry manufactured a happy smile for them.

"We're being awful quiet, like papa said," Tommy reported.

"You're good children! Is there anything here for your lunch?"

"Papa left us apples."

"An' bread." Jenny pointed a tiny finger.

"Oh, yes, and milk."

That was something but it would not do for every day—and Mrs. George might be sick a long time. The neighbors could not be asked to take over five children; they had heavy responsibilities of their own. Nor should the two older sisters be kept away from school. What could Miss Davis do for these five children?

Cherry whispered her question to Nurse Cornish as they finished taking the sick woman's temperature, pulse, and respiration, and marked these on the record.

Mary Cornish looked troubled. "Maybe there are relatives who could help out, or take the children into their own homes. Mrs. George," she gently caught the woman's wandering attention. "Mrs. George. Have you or your husband any relatives in the city?"

The woman weakly shook her head. "Canada," she whispered. "My children—will you—?"

"Don't worry," the nurse reassured her. "We'll send in a housekeeper to look after your children, and you, too. Now lie back, my dear, I'm going to give you an injection—"

"Can't pay—"

"The city will pay the housekeeper. Ssh, now." While Cherry swabbed the woman's thin arm for the needle Mary Cornish held ready, she thought with relief of that housekeeper service. Without it, these five little tykes might have to go temporarily to orphanages, hardly a happy experience. "This isn't charity," Cherry realized silently. "This is keeping a family together. Mrs. George will certainly recover faster, knowing her children are looked out for!"

Mrs. George required a good deal of care. Then Nurse Cornish and Cherry examined the five youngsters. They warned them to stay out of their mother's room, explaining that their mother had an infectious disease and what that meant. But they might stand in the doorway and talk with her. The children nodded solemnly. Miss Cornish left a tonic prescription for Tommy's cold, to be filled free of charge at the clinic, and a note for Mr. George to be at home at nine tomorrow morning. She would return then to give him instructions.

"Mr. George will have to give me the facts about the family tomorrow," Mary Cornish said with a sigh. "His wife is too sick to talk. And I had planned to teach the family today how to take care of their patient, too. Oh, dear! Well, I guess we've done everything we can on this visit, haven't we? I'll have to do more on the next calls."

Cherry sterilized all the nursing instruments, repacked her bag, then she and Mary Cornish scrubbed their hands. They spent several more minutes cheering up the children and chocolate bars came out of Nurse Cornish's pockets for them. When they again were out on the dark, rickety stairs, Cherry was sober and silent.

"Don't feel badly," Nurse Cornish said over her shoulder.

"I'm not," Cherry replied. "I was just thinking how awful it would be for the Georges if we and the clinic and the housekeeper service *weren't* here!"

The next case, a treatment, proved to be a welcome contrast.

Mr. Xenos, an elderly tailor, had cut his hand on his sewing machine, and it had become infected. He fumed because, with his hand bandaged, he could not work, and he called on all the gods to persuade Miss Cornish not to change the dressing.

She explained patiently that the hand might never heal unless it was kept medicated and scrupulously clean.

"Is no good, no good!" he insisted furiously.

"What's no good?" Miss Cornish smiled, struggling to dress the hand anyway.

"This white rag what goes round and round on my hand! Can't sew, can't earn! I tear it off when you go!"

Cherry and Mary Cornish stared at the indignant old man. Then the nurse gave Cherry a glance and said to Mr. Xenos:

"If you'll leave the bandage on, I'll bring you my other uniforms to be fixed."

"Aha!"

"And if you let me bandage it next time, I'll—I'll bring you my coat to be lengthened."

"Aha!"

"And if you let me bandage it next week, I'll—"

"Wait!" thundered the old man. His face had altered. "Is very kind. Is very nice. You wish to show I need the bandage. You wish for me to make the money. But do you think I charge *you*? No." He bristled, then resignedly held out his hand. "I am convinced. I will leave it on, your bandage, by golly!"

A few minutes later two amused nurses entered a musty drug store and perched at a soda fountain for lunch. Mary Cornish smiled at Cherry.

"Now you've had a sample. Do you think you're going to like being a visiting nurse?"

Cherry tossed back her dark curls, and her black eyes sparkled. "I not only think so—I know so! And I certainly am going to learn about people!"

And she began to think in earnest of having her own district.

CHAPTER VI

Cherry's Own District

ALMOST ANY EVENING, FOR THE ENSUING MONTH, THE Spencer Club could be found earnestly practicing bag technique, or comparing notes on Chinatown versus the Bronx, or rubbing aching legs with alcohol.

"Thirty flights of stairs today!" Gwen groaned regularly.

"Let's review the lecture on family budgeting," Mai Lee, sleepy but conscientious, proposed at least twice a week.

"And the new lecture on the care of new babies. I'm rusty," Josie confessed. "Wake up, Vivian. Poor Vivi, you can't fall asleep *yet*."

Cherry giggled. "What a mad round of riotous living."

They were taking turns at cooking, too, not wishing to impose on good-humored Bertha Larsen. It seemed to Cherry that the six of them ran as fast as they could, all day every day, to get through their many duties. There was no time but Sunday for sight-seeing, and on Sundays they luxuriously slept. The breakneck schedule left Cherry breathless but satisfied, for this work was rewarding.

After going out several times more with Nurse Cornish, Cherry had then had the benefit of Miss Davis's supervision on further field trips. For several weeks now, as the weather grew colder, Cherry had been going out all by herself on carefully selected cases. She made one or two blunders, being too sympathetic with an overdemanding family, and once bathing the wrong patient. But, on the whole, Cherry and her fellow nurses were developing real skill in dealing with their families.

"Wish we had time some evening to get back to that Paradiso restaurant," Vivian said plaintively, as she and Cherry dried dishes.

"It's quite a walk. The Ames feet wouldn't stand for it."

Vivian giggled. "We're floaters—why can't we just float down there?"

Bertha called in, "The gold curtains are ready to hang! Who wants to help?"

"Who wants to put on a final coat of paint?" Gwen's shout came from the opposite end of the apartment.

Their apartment was beginning to shape up. The living room would have been a credit even to their mothers. More lamps, a wall full of Mai Lee's Chinese prints, and a handsome extra clock of Ann's on the mantel, "made the room human," as Vivian said.

The back parlor was brightly papered now as Cherry had suggested, courtesy of the Spencer Club, not the landlord, and the furniture painted blue. The girls had paste in their hair and blue-stained hands for days, but they agreed the room had turned out fresh and cheerful. Josie pleaded for a canary, then for a dog, and finally for a cat, but she was outvoted.

"Only these three poky bedrooms," Cherry fretted, "still have that rented, cheerless look."

"What's the difference?" Gwen said. 'We're in them only to sleep. Our eyes are closed so we can't see 'em, anyway."

The bedrooms were hopeless, they all admitted. Besides, their spare money had run out. They decided the best solution was to ignore the bedrooms.

"Oh!"

"What's the matter, Cherry?"

"We never did return Mrs. Jenkins's gingerbread!"

"How could we return it, when we ate it?" Josie blinked.

"Silly, Cherry means we ought to reciprocate. Let's fill her basket—we've kept it a disgracefully long time!—let's fill it with—with—what?"

"I'll bring rice cakes and preserved ginger from Chinatown," Mai Lee suggested. "We simply haven't time to do any extra cooking, you know that."

"Bring some for the janitor's wife, too," Bertha asked. "She's been nice, she does so many little things to help us."

Being career women certainly did crowd their time. One of the time-consumers was traveling around this enormous city. Every one of the girls spent an hour on the subway getting from home to her center, and another hour in the evening getting back again. Besides, from center to headquarters for more lectures, and from center out to the far-flung districts, meant crisscrossing back and forth on buses and streetcars. At first Cherry just sat (or stood) and stared curiously at these hordes of people, never seeing the same face twice. Presently she learned to utilize her traveling time by reading, finding newspapers best; thus she became well informed on current events.

"How to turn a liability into an asset," Cherry mused. "Or, The Straphanger's Reward."

But on one bus she caught regularly, Cherry had difficulty concentrating on her newspaper. The driver was always so cross that Cherry listened in a kind of horrified fascination.

"Step lively, I ain't got all day!"

"Naw, no transfers to Northern Drive! Whatcha want for a nickel?"

"I told ya I can't let ya off over there! A bus can't go *anywheres*!"

Passengers trembled at his gibes. Cherry shied away from him herself. The bus stopped and started apparently at the cranky driver's whim, while regular bus stops went shooting by. The driver jolted the bus to a stop in a way that set the passengers' teeth on edge. It was so awful it was rather interesting. Cherry decided he probably had stomach ulcers or an unhappy married life, to make him behave so ferociously. His name was Smith and she was sufficiently impressed to write home to Hilton about him.

"Whatcha think this is, yer private taxi?"

"If ya don't like it, get out an' walk!"

Driver Smith, although an unavoidable evil, had a sort of showmanship. Riding with him might be hair-raising but it was never dull.

At the center Cherry felt that she had belonged there for years. Bobbie and Miss Davis looked as familiar to her by now as first cousins. Mrs. Berkey, the assistant supervisor who appeared somewhat forbidding at first, turned out to be as friendly and helpful as the rest of the office. Sitting next to Mary Cornish at one of the long tables, with witty Dolly Click on her other side, Cherry felt warmly at home, though she was still only a floater. She did want her own district. Especially when the morning mail from patients was distributed, and there were no letters for the floaters, did Cherry long to have a district and families of her very own.

The day finally came. Miss Davis said:

"It's one of our most difficult neighborhoods, Miss Ames, because it's spread out and there's no transportation out there."

"I'm a good walker," Cherry said stoutly.

"Also," the young supervisor hesitated, "it's quite poor and you'll have to use your wits more than once."

Cherry was puzzled but not dismayed. She wanted to hurry right out to her district and see what it was like. But Dorothy Davis advised her to read the district's case records first. She added:

"A very good nurse handled the area for several years, until she became ill and resigned. You'll find that she has done a lot of good teaching, and also paved the way for you in good will."

Cherry was grateful to hear that.

It was noon before she had hastily studied case records and confided the good news to Gwen—Bertha and Josie had left for the field. Then she started out for—triumph!—her own district.

Half an hour later, after a roundabout route and consulting her pocket map, Cherry stood at the street where her district began.

"Well, this is a pleasant surprise!"

Although an isolated tenement building rose up here and there, mostly there were rows of modest, frame houses. Wide stretches of ground or vacant lots separated these. Cherry strolled down the central street, passing garages, a grocery, a school, trees blowing in the October wind. Not many people were about. How peaceful it was!

Cherry had to tramp for a long time, searching many blocks of small cottages for the address of her first call of the day. Some of the side streets were only dirt roads and so lonely as to seem in the depths of the country. Cherry could recall she was in New York City only by glancing at the pale, distant silhouettes of skyscrapers and bridges, or hearing frequent planes overhead. Then a stretch of two or three citified blocks would crop up again.

Suddenly, as she turned a corner, she came to something that caught her attention. It was a once-elegant Victorian house, almost a mansion, fenced in and half hidden behind thickly overgrown trees. The few windows which were visible had concealing lace curtains. On some windows, shutters were tightly closed. In the deep stillness surrounding the place, there was no sign of life.

"How odd," Cherry thought. "That old house is still beautiful and—well, mysterious."

She wondered for a moment whether, in her excitement over having her own district, she was romanticizing. But the Victorian house, fenced off and some distance from any neighbors, did have a distinct atmosphere of its own.

"I'll ask a tradesman about it," Cherry noted mentally, and hurried along to locate the family who had sent out an emergency call for the nurse.

The address led her to a two-family wooden house, well-kept but colorless on the outside. "Persson," her call list read. Cherry rang a doorbell, righted her hat on her curls, hoped she would be even half as welcome and useful as Mary Cornish was on her district, and started expectantly up the stairs.

The door flew open and a plump, blue-eyed woman in a house dress beamed at her.

"Oh, the nurse is here! We are so glad! Come in!"

"I'm Miss Ames," Cherry smiled. "I hope you haven't been waiting long," and she stepped into the Persson household.

She found herself in a home she never could have guessed at, looking at this ordinary house from the street. This Swedish-American household was one of the most inviting, shipshape interiors she had ever been in: simple, handmade furniture of bleached wood, hand-loomed fabrics in serene, cool blues and greens, an air of calm and spaciousness. Over the homemade brick fireplace hung six glass squares, beautifully decorated in red and gold, and printed in Swedish with family names, cities, and birth dates.

Mrs. Persson—it was pronounced Pierson, she said—smiled at Cherry's interest.

"Those are all the members of our family. It is an old custom with us. See, one for my husband Seth, one for Ingrid—that's me—our children Jon, Constant, and Inga—and one for Uncle Gustave."

Cherry, charmed by such birth certificates, fished her family forms out of her black bag and wrote down the list of family members, since this was a new case.

"Who is ill, Mrs. Persson?"

"Uncle Gustave. I think—sit down, ssh, I tell you something"—she lowered her voice and Cherry thought Mrs. Persson had the bluest eyes she had ever seen—"I think Uncle Gustave is not really sick."

"Then what—?"

"I think Uncle Gustave is unhappy. So unhappy he gets sick from it."

She talked on, and Cherry tactfully interpolated the required questions needed to take the family history. Cherry's pencil flew as the story came out.

Uncle Gustave had come to the United States when he was a young man, bringing his small nephew Seth with him. Good builders were needed to help young American towns grow into cities, and people from other nations were invited to bring their effort and their skills, and become Americans. Mrs. Persson's parents had arrived earlier, to build ships for American trading. She had been born and raised and educated here. Only the sea-blue of her eyes, a faint singsong in her voice and a demureness of manner showed that her parents had been transplanted Americans.

"It was not easy for my people to leave Sweden," Mrs. Persson told Cherry earnestly. "They were substantial, prosperous people there. They had to leave behind parents and home and learn a new language, and start life all over again. But they believed in this new country and"—she smiled—"immigrants, too, were pioneers."

Mr. Persson was a master carpenter, their eldest son Jon was training to be a shipbuilder, Constant and Inga attended high school. Uncle Gustave, who had been a "carpetect"—an architect who built houses with his own hands—now was too old to work. Mrs. Persson led the way in to see him, murmuring that close to a hundred of Uncle Gustave's stone houses sheltered families all through New York State and Connecticut, and that he was heartbroken because he was too old to build any more.

Uncle Gustave's room was another surprise for Cherry. In the midst of worktables, tools, blueprints, and neat rows of gadgets sat a small, brown-haired man, with the same very blue eyes. He rose politely from his cot to greet Cherry and his niece, then wearily sat down again.

"Well, now, Mr. Persson," said Cherry cheerfully, "let's see what we can do to make you stronger. From the looks of you," she fibbed, "I'm sure we can do a great deal."

The doctor's report said: secondary anemia, heart murmur, recurrent nosebleeds. Cherry knew that these physical symptoms could have emotional causes. "Distress signals?" she wondered.

She checked Uncle Gustave over, with Mrs. Persson's help. Then she gently changed the awkward, cotton dressing with which Mrs. Persson had checked his nosebleed this morning. Cherry showed them both how to stop a nosebleed, instructed Uncle Gustave to drink lemon juice, hold his head back, use ice, and rest. She left a packet of medicated cotton for them. After this first visit, Cherry would do as little nursing as possible, for she wanted the family to be self-reliant.

"How long did Uncle Gustave's nose bleed this morning?"

"Almost an hour," the little man said angrily. "Now I feel weak as a cat. Bah."

No wonder, Cherry thought, after losing all that blood. Moreover, an anemic person could not afford any loss of blood.

"What made the nosebleed start? Do you know?"

"Nothing made it start," Uncle Gustave said in even greater disgust.

"Yah, I think there was a reason," Mrs. Persson murmured thoughtfully. "He was making a—a something, and he needed a special kind of screws. They are very expensive and there was no money to get them. Our boy

Constant said he would sell his ice skates, but Uncle Gustave—"

"I do not take away the boy's skates!" the little old man snapped. "He is the star of the ice carnival at the high school last winter. But it's like this, nurse. For three days now I build this little machine, and over and over, for no screws, it falls apart in my hands. It is enough to make one cry."

There was a silence. Cherry sympathized with this craftsman, his intelligent hands threatened by age and lack of funds. Why, the whole point of his life was being taken away from him!

"What are you making?" she asked.

Brightening, he showed her the tableful of his inventions, which ranged from the extremely ingenious to a hilarious device for washing dishes—a chore which Uncle Gustave apparently detested. Then, suddenly tired, he admitted he had better lie down.

In the other room Cherry worked out a diet for him and explained to Mrs. Persson how to plan and vary it, within the family's limited means. As Cherry prepared to go, Mrs. Persson said shyly:

"Please, won't you stay and have coffee and kondis with me?"

"Why, thank you! But—but—you know, it's a policy of our service not to accept gifts, unless they are for the Visiting Nurse Service itself. Thank you just the same for your hospitality," Cherry smiled.

Mrs. Persson flushed. "I cannot pay you very much. Fifty cents, perhaps."

Then Cherry understood. This family of six, with only one earner, could not afford to pay at all. Mrs. Persson's offer of refreshments was her way of saying "thank you" to the nurse. It might be ungracious not to accept.

"But there is no charge, Mrs. Persson," Cherry tried to reassure her.

"But I should like you to stay! Please. Uncle Gustave will come in, too. We will have a little party," Mrs. Persson said eagerly. Then she hesitated and looked lonesomely into Cherry's eyes. "You see, except for the minister, when he can come from Brooklyn, we have almost no company. There are no other Swedish-American families in this neighborhood."

"But why," Cherry asked in amazement, "shouldn't you be friends with people who *didn't* originally come from Sweden?"

Mrs. Persson knit her brows. "We would like to. Only I think we are shy and the French family downstairs are shy. And the people across the street, with the German name, maybe they think we don't want to be friends." Suddenly she laughed. "Isn't it foolish? But all our children go to school together, they are friends."

Cherry, who came from the friendly Midwest, was puzzled at people living as next-door neighbors and not knowing one another. She said as warmly as she could:

"Well, I should like very much to stay for your coffee party! What is *kondis*?"

"Pastry. Uncle Gustave! Come in! Miss Ames is staying and we are having a party!"

Mrs. Persson's cheeks were pink with excitement. She bustled about, brewing fragrant coffee, setting the table with elaborate care. Cherry helped her bring in little cakes and a crimson sauce made of lingonberries. Uncle Gustave was already at the table.

Cherry thoroughly enjoyed their party. She was surprised and touched to find Mrs. Persson hungry for news of other families, and how they lived. So Cherry told about Hilton, described their house, and talked of her brother Charlie who was studying to become an engineer.

Uncle Gustave nodded approval. "Constant and Inga, both of them, they want to be engineers. But Inga should stay home and cook."

"Ah, Uncle Gustave, you and your old-country ideas!" Mrs. Persson cried. "Inga shall be an engineer, and a good one. Miss Ames, don't you say so, too?"

Cherry was reluctant to take sides but her dark eyes sparkled with sympathy for Inga. There was no need to take sides, however. They heard a running on the stairs, muffled laughter, and two tall, nice-looking youngsters came bursting into the room. These were Inga and Constant, school pins on their lapels, arms full of textbooks.

"Hi, Mother! Better, Uncle Gussie?" They grinned at Cherry, waiting to be introduced. "Who's this you're feeding *kondis* to? You must like her!" they teased.

"She deserves *kondis*," their mother twinkled back at them. She performed the introductions and invited them to "my party." Cherry stayed on a while longer, chuckling at Inga's groans over algebra, and Connie's funny description of three neighborhood boys running their jalopy on eighteen cents' worth of gasoline and a cupful of mouthwash.

"The mouthwash works fine," Connie declared, reaching for his sixth cake. "But we expect the jalopy to turn around any day and deliver a toothpaste commercial."

Cherry had to leave. Other people were waiting for her. As she got her hat, and the party broke up, she saw Uncle Gustave's face grow clouded again. He trudged back into his own small room.

"Have to give Uncle Gustave a new lease on life," Cherry thought. "Not medicine but psychology. Have to find a solution for him, somehow."

She took Connie aside and said she would like to present his uncle with the special screws he needed. The boy shook his head.

"They're really expensive," he explained. "Thanks a lot, anyhow."

"I'll figure out some way," Cherry muttered.

She thanked Mrs. Persson cordially, promised to get in touch with them soon again, and left.

During the rest of the afternoon, Cherry visited six more homes and talked to dozens of new people. Her head whirled with impressions. Each home was different, and interesting. She was so excited at exploring her district, and worked so hard giving nursing care and teaching, that it was long past five o'clock—six-ten, in fact—when Cherry hiked the long way back to the bus line.

Only then, as the Victorian mansion loomed up ahead in the shadows, did Cherry remember she had omitted to ask about the place. Passing it now, the only sound was the night wind. The house was dark, in its tangle of blowing, autumn garden. No, there was a light in one window. Cherry stood on tiptoe beside the fence but could make out nothing.

"Mustn't forget to ask someone," she thought, starting on again. "Heavens, but I'm going to be late for supper! And, oh, how tired I am. But what a day, what a day this has been!"

CHAPTER VII

The Mysterious Mansion

MR. JONAS'S GROCERY AND DELICATESSEN, CHERRY DIScovered, was the place to learn anything she wanted to know about her district. Housewives shopped here in the morning for bread and baby foods. Working people dropped in at six for the hasty makings of a supper. The policeman of Cherry's district, Officer O'Brien, and the high school crowd would come by as late as eleven at night for sandwiches. So Mr. Jonas saw everyone, knew everyone, and—since he was a kindly soul—listened to everybody's life history and troubles.

The old man was willing to confide to Cherry, because she was district nurse, why the Bennett boy was in disgrace and what was really wrong with Mrs. Castillo's baby. He was just as likely to discourse to her on literature, the history of the Jews, and the moral writings of Spinoza, if she had time. Learned books lay on top of pickle barrels and she found a music score fallen into the dried-prune bin.

The only thing that kept his mind on business was Mama Jonas's matriarchal form and deep, deliberate voice calling from the back of the long, narrow shop where she made dill pickles and potato salad—

"Papa! That's enough philosophy for today! The hot pastrami and corned beef are scorching!"

"Ah, Mama. We do not live by bread alone."

"You won't even live by pastrami alone if you don't stop your talking."

"*Liebchen*, I am only explaining to Miss Ames the grammar of classical Hebrew—"

"Miss Ames needs grammar like she needs a hole in the head. Don't you know she's busy? And what did you give her for her lunch?"

Mama, roly-poly but commanding, marched up the aisle between shelves and counter to confront tall, thin Papa.

"Abraham! You only gave her a cheese sandwich? On this cold, rainy day, cheese he gives her yet! Have you no judgment? Come, child, I'll give you hot chicken broth and dumplings."

Cherry, amused and enjoying this, protested: "But I like this sandwich just fine, Mrs. Jonas. I ordered it!"

Mr. Jonas peered at her out of dreamy blue eyes. "It is not nice to contradict your elders, darling."

Mama firmly took the sandwich away from Cherry. "I have raised two good sons and a good daughter on chicken broth—not cheese sandwiches. You will eat chicken broth."

As she strode away for the broth, Mr. Jonas twinkled at Cherry. "With our people, one obeys the mama and the papa. My wife's mother is still alive and believe me, darling, she rules both Mama and me with an iron hand."

Cherry chuckled. "And do you rule your children with an iron hand?"

"Why, certainly! Even though they are grown and Jack is a doctor, Ben is a musician, and Ruthie has a millinery shop, *still*—! They are still our children, aren't they? Mama and I see to it that they behave themselves. Or else."

"They behave themselves or else they should drop dead!" Mama had returned with a plate of steaming broth. "Now, little Miss Nurse, eat this. On such a day, cheese already!"

There was nothing for it but to "obey the elders." Cherry ate obediently and the broth did warm her through. She had never before met such strict, energetic, sharp-tongued, warmhearted, and unabashedly sentimental people as the Jonases. Now, she remembered, she must ask about that old mansion.

Mr. Jonas nodded. "A corner house. The only one in such an old-fashioned style around here."

"Oh, you know it, then!"

"Yes. That's the Gregory place."

"Can you tell me about it, Mr. Jonas?"

The old man blinked his blue eyes. "For eighteen years I have known that house. . . . You are quick, to notice something strange there. Many people pass by and think it is just another old house."

"But I—I—felt something," Cherry confessed. "There's an atmosphere—"

"Of sadness. Of secrets. Yes, one can feel it. Well," Mr. Jonas cleared his throat, "I will tell you what little I know."

Eighteen years ago, when he first opened this grocery, a pretty young woman came in alone late one night. She ordered a great many supplies, paid by check, and arranged to have regular weekly orders delivered to her house. The check was signed "Mary Gregory" and the bank honored it.

"She would not talk about herself, or about anything," Mr. Jonas said, recalling that long-ago visit. "Very nice but very reserved. Shy, I think. And so young, so pretty! But there was something sad about her that made me feel sorry for her even then."

No one in the neighborhood had known anything about her, Mr. Jonas continued. The house was rumored to belong to a wealthy family named Gregory. But they had long since moved to mid-town New York, and the house had been closed up for many years. Then this young woman had come, all alone, opened the house, and started living there.

"For about a month Miss Gregory—I say 'miss' because she wore no wedding ring," Mr. Jonas went on to Cherry, "traded with me by leaving a note on her doorstep with the order, and a check. I thought nothing of this, I thought she was busy moving in and getting her house in order, I thought soon she would come into my grocery again." The old man shrugged. "Then, in one note, Miss Gregory asked me to buy meat for her from the butcher. And to send it along with the rest of her regular weekly order. This I did, never suspecting what it meant."

"And what did it mean?" Cherry breathed.

"That I was never to see her again. Every week for eighteen years my errand boy goes on Thursday to pick up the basket on her doorstep. In it is a check for last week's order and a note telling what she needs. Friday I pack up the food and my boy goes back to leave it on her step. For eighteen years no one has seen Mary Gregory."

She was never seen to set foot outside her door. She was not even seen on the porches or in the garden, although some neighborhood people said they had glimpsed a white, ghostly figure on an upstairs balcony on summer evenings. No visitors were ever seen to enter or leave. The postman reported that the only mail which came for her was from a bank, utility and coal companies, and department stores. If neighbors rang her doorbell, no one answered.

Cherry leaned against a wall lined with canned goods and blinked in her own turn.

"But why—?"

"Who knows why?"

"Wouldn't Officer O'Brien know?"

"Even he does not go in there. He says, 'Leave her in peace, that is what she wants.' "

"But suppose she fell sick, or had an accident, all alone in there!" Cherry cried.

Mr. Jonas shook his head. "We all think of that. The whole neighborhood feels bad about Mary Gregory. Or used to. Not so many people know, any more. The old ones have moved away or forgotten, many others pay no attention. She is like a legend."

Cherry sputtered. "No one at all ever sees her?"

"Wait. Excuse me. I told you one thing wrong, darling. She does let the furnace man in. He does repairs, too. But the furnace man never sees her. It is always by notes, like with me. The same way with the plumber, and when a man went to put in a new stove. Once a year, a man, dressed very well, goes in. *He* stays a few hours. I guess he is her lawyer or banker or something. But never, never, does anyone else see her."

Cherry murmured, "And you still send her food every week?"

"Yes. For eighteen solitary years, the poor soul. And she was so young, so pretty!"

Why had Mary Gregory retired from life? Cherry went out of Mr. Jonas's grocery-delicatessen shaken.

This was not the time to think about the mysterious recluse, though. Her lunch period was over and Cherry had sick calls awaiting her, including a child ill of scarlet fever. That was a communicable disease and could easily start an epidemic!

"I'll have to do some pretty sound teaching," Cherry realized and quickened her pace.

The Terrell cottage was spick-and-span outside and in. Mrs. Terrell, an anxious-eyed young woman, had three small children tugging on her skirts. Jimmy, aged nine, lay sick in one of the bedrooms.

"The doctor says we're in quarantine, nurse," the mother said anxiously, "but I'm not sure about what it means nor all the things to do."

"I'll show you, Mrs. Terrell," Cherry calmed her. "I know you have your hands awfully full. I'll keep coming to help you until you and I get this thing under control."

"Thank goodness!" Mrs. Terrell said. "I certainly wouldn't want anybody else's children to get scarlet fever. Mrs. Kramer upstairs says my three youngest ones are sure to catch it, living in the same house with Jimmy." She looked at Cherry in helpless appeal.

"Now, don't you believe such old wives' tales. There's no reason why these other three"—Cherry stopped to grin down at the round-eyed toddlers—"shouldn't be safe, provided you're careful."

"Oh, I'll do anything you say, nurse, anything!"

"Well, let's start, shall we? Will you get some clean newspapers, please? And I'd like to wash my hands."

Cherry scrubbed up, tied on her apron, and peeked into the bedroom at the patient. Small Jimmy was hunched up in bed, asleep. His cheeks and forehead were pebbly with rash, and he breathed with difficulty. Cherry decided not to waken him: the first step was to teach his mother safety methods.

Back in the kitchen with Mrs. Terrell, Cherry began asking questions. (Cherry, like the rest of the visiting nurses, had routinely received various antitoxins so that she could nurse contagious disease without becoming ill herself.) The doctor had told Mrs. Terrell that Jimmy must be kept isolated. His father and the other children were to be kept away from him. The children were not to go to kindergarten nor to leave the house, until the quarantine was lifted. However, Mr. Terrell was permitted to go out of the house to work.

"But *how* do I keep Jim isolated?" the young mother asked the nurse in bewilderment. "The doctor told me some, but I'm all confused—"

Cherry told her how to arrange Jimmy's room so Mrs. Terrell could take care of him without spreading the disease. First, take away the pictures and rugs, to simplify the problem of cleaning when the illness was over. The curtains were washable, so Cherry said these could remain. The closet was contaminated because, Mrs. Terrell reported, Jimmy had hung his clothes with those of the other children; Cherry said to leave the closet undisturbed, and not to use anything in it. She asked Mrs. Terrell to bring into Jimmy's room any extra, small table she had, to hold a pitcher and basin for the mother's own use in washing her hands. Then she lined a wastebasket with newspaper, showing Mrs. Terrell how to do it. Cherry advised her to buy or borrow a bedpan, to keep the bathroom safe for the rest of the family. A dishpan of soapy water, placed on newspapers, would have to be left outside Jimmy's door to receive soiled dishes, and a wash boiler to receive soiled linen.

"It isn't as bad as it sounds," Cherry encouraged. "But you must remember that everything that comes out of Jimmy's room is a possible germ carrier. When it leaves the room it must be boiled or disinfected before it touches anything else."

"I'm going to write all of this down," the young mother said nervously. "I'll just get pencil and paper from Jimmy's schoolbooks—" She started to go into the sickroom, with the obvious intention of bringing the pencil and paper back into the living room. Cherry gasped and stopped her. Then she carefully explained all over again.

"Look here," said Cherry. She saw a piece of the children's chalk on the living-room floor. With it she drew a thick, white line outside Jimmy's door. "This line will remind you."

Mrs. Terrell smiled weakly. "It certainly will," and she was calmer after that.

"Soap and water, lots and lots of it for everything, especially your hands, Mrs. Terrell," Cherry instructed. "A tray for toilet articles. A tray for medicines. A clean smock to put on when you enter Jimmy's room, and to leave on a hook beside his door, so you won't carry out germs on your clothes. When you're carrying anything out of his room, leave the smock on *but*—don't touch anything! If you must touch, for dumping something, for instance, use squares of newspaper. Remember your hands are contaminated. Tie all garbage and waste in clean newspapers, and burn it. Now, is it all clear? Can you remember to do all this?"

Jimmy's mother nodded, furiously scribbling down these instructions. Then, at Cherry's request, she brought a covered pitcher of water, a glass, and a glass of fruit juice. They shooed the three toddlers away and went in to see Jimmy.

Poor Jimmy's freckles scarcely showed under the rash. He woke up to stare at Cherry and say gratingly, "Sore throat."

"Hello, Jimmy," Cherry said. "Your mother and I are going to get you well quickly, you'll see! Now here's a pitcher of water, right where you can reach it. Doctor wants you to drink all the water you can, Jim. But wait, please, until I've taken your temperature."

She counted the little boy's temperature, pulse, and respiration, and wrote them down. She showed Mrs. Terrell how to keep Jimmy clean and comfortable in bed.

"I don't feel very sick," Jimmy said.

"No, you're not very sick," Cherry told him. "You won't be, because your mother will follow instructions exactly. Better get some paper handkerchiefs, too, Mrs. Terrell; they can be burned. Then, when Jimmy is well again, you'll clean everything—furniture, floor, curtains, shades, blankets, clothes—with soap and water. You'll air his room for a couple of days. And you'll take his mattress, and any clothes that can't be washed, outdoors and give them a thorough sunning."

"No fumigation?" Mrs. Terrell said in relief.

Cherry explained that soap and water, sun and air are the best disinfectants. She did sympathize with this overworked mother. Combating contagious disease was a great nuisance—or any disease, for that matter.

"It's a lot simpler to stay well," Cherry reflected as, at last, thoroughly scrubbed herself, she left the Terrell cottage. "Oh, yes, must remember to send a report to the Department of Health on this case."

She stopped at the corner drugstore to catch her breath and phone back to the center. No, Bobbie said, there were no new calls for her.

"And a good thing! Today's call list is long enough."

She sat down at the counter for a quick coke. The sixteen-year-old soda fountain boy eyed her curiously as she sipped it.

"Excuse me, but aren't you the new district nurse?"

Cherry smiled, admitted it, and told him her name.

"My name's Joe Baxter. What do you think of our neighborhood?"

"I like it a lot. Lots of nice people living around here."

Joe Baxter looked pleased. "Sure, lots of okay people in most neighborhoods, I guess. But our neighborhood has something special."

"The view of the Manhattan skyline?"

"No. We have a mystery around here."

"A mystery?" Cherry half smiled. "In this quiet neighborhood? You're joking. You're trying to play a trick on me, I'll bet."

"No, I'm not." Joe Baxter looked at her soberly. "Say, haven't you seen that mysterious old house?"

Cherry stiffened. "You mean the Gregory house? Yes."

The boy leaned toward her on the counter. "Well, there's a lady living in there but nobody ever sees her. It's the craziest thing. Everybody says she's a witch or something. I saw her, though, when I was a little shaver."

"You saw her? You talked to her?" Cherry breathed.

Joe Baxter wiped the marble of the soda fountain.

"Yeah, years ago. Miss Gregory used to let us neighborhood kids play in her yard. She'd smile at us through the window. Sometimes she'd even talk to us, a little." There was a faraway look in the boy's eyes. "I guess she'd still let the children nowadays come. But for the last couple of years, they haven't gone near her."

"Why not?"

"Well, things began to change. In the last year or two, some of the kids"—Joe frowned—"said they saw strange goings-on at night. Shadows of witches dancing against the blinds, or something. It gave them the shivers."

"Did you ever see them?" Cherry challenged.

"No'm. But all the kids say it's so. Anyhow, their parents began telling them to stay away. So they stopped playing in her yard."

Cherry listened to this with pity for Mary Gregory. The recluse must have needed the children around her, if she had encouraged them to come. Now even that small solace was lost to her. In the last year or two, Joe Baxter said. That was odd . . .

"In fact," Joe said, his eyes round, "lots of mothers tell their children if they don't behave, Mary Gregory will do something awful to them. The kids are plenty scared of her and that scary house. They say you really can see witches' shadows. I'm not joking. There must be something spooky in there. They say it—well, it looks like a gallows."

"A gallows?"

"Yes, a hangman's gallows."

Cherry was impressed but outraged all the same. Using that lonely creature as a bogeyman! She vowed to herself that she would find out more about it all.

"But not today. Heavens, what a list of calls I have. I mustn't even think about Mary Gregory this afternoon. Have to get myself in a more cheerful frame of mind, too, so I can cheer up my patients."

Nurse Ames had a lively afternoon. In a dimly lit apartment, she found tall, lean Boris Sergeyevsky and his very blonde wife, both coming down with influenza, both in long, black kimonos, gesturing with long cigarette holders and offering her tea with lemon, from their samovar. "Everybody wants to feed me," Cherry chuckled to herself. Grateful, all these people wanted to give her something; having nothing else to give, they wanted to share their limited food with her.

Next came a visit to a Greek-American family in a kitchen strewn with confetti and wilting white roses. For two years they had saved to give their Phoebe a glorious wedding. Yesterday Phoebe was wed, there was a feast, and the entire family now had an acute stomachache. Cherry proffered congratulations and remedies. They gratefully pressed roses and Grecian wine on her—"more refreshments! I must look hungry"—but she wriggled out of accepting.

Cherry thought, though, what fun it would be to spread this wine, Mrs. Persson's *kondis* and lingonberries, the Russians' lemon *tshay,* Mama Jonas's chicken broth and dumplings, and Mama Mediterraneo's *pasta* all on one huge table, and invite them all to partake.

"Say, that really is a thought!" But she had to hurry along to many more calls.

The last case of the afternoon Cherry found the most appealing. She had treated Miss Culver only once before. The all-day rain had stopped and, though it was dusk now, a silver afterglow hung in the sky.

A slight woman opened the door to Cherry. Against the second-story windows that gleamed with the curious light she stood silhouetted.

"Come look here!" the woman said eagerly, after the briefest of greetings. She led Cherry to the windows, to look down at the shabby street. People, houses, cars were bathed in shadowy silver, like figures in a dream. "Just look!"

Cherry smiled at this imaginative woman. "Yes, it's beautiful," and she thought, "Not many people would see beauty on an everyday street. Especially one they have to look at every day."

"It's different every hour of the day," Miss Culver said thoughtfully. "And from week to week, as the earth moves around the sun and the seasons change, my street changes into something new and different."

Cherry looked at Miss Culver with sympathy. The daughter of an old family who had fallen on evil times, she had not bemoaned her fate but quietly had become a private secretary. She had devoted her life to taking care of her parents. Now that they were dead, she was alone. Recently her frail body had broken down, exhausted after years of work.

But nothing could quench her spirit. Living on a pittance, Cherry knew that Miss Culver limited herself to the most Spartan diet, so that she would have a few pennies left to put in the collection plate at church on Sundays. She was fighting to hold on to her standards. Her shabby one-room apartment might have been pitiful in another owner's hands, but Miss Culver had made it a gracious home. A Duncan Phyfe antique sofa told of better days; its carefully mended upholstery mutely testified to her determination. Well-chosen books, borrowed without cost from the public library, lay on her table, beside a lovingly polished, old silver teapot. A chair and footstool were drawn up to the window, a tray-table held a few odd pieces of fragile china and a tiny radio—"so that I can have music and a view with my meals," Miss Culver had explained.

Miss Culver herself was always dainty as a miniature and bore herself like a princess. Cherry respectfully regarded her as a triumphant soldier.

"Well, let's see how you are today." Cherry smiled. Miss Culver was convalescing from an attack of bronchitis. Her real trouble was need of a long rest.

"My throat is almost healed, thank you. But I still feel so weak and tired. However, I'm sure this is only temporary. I will get back my strength. I will return to my position again."

"I know you will," Cherry encouraged her. "Just don't try it prematurely, Miss Culver. Be patient and rest."

She wished Miss Culver could afford to go away on a vacation. Her only recreation was to take short walks. It must be lonely, sitting in this room without much to occupy her. Cherry recalled Mrs. Crump's saying how it irked her to do nothing, and Uncle Gustave's unhappiness at being idle. Miss Culver, too, needed something interesting and satisfying to do, while her strength slowly returned.

Out on the street, Cherry was thinking so hard about Miss Culver that she walked beyond the bus stop. And Uncle Gustave, too . . . she still had not solved his problem. Then Cherry realized where her feet were leading her: to a place she had intended for weeks to visit, but had always been too busy to get to—the settlement house.

"I really ought to get my people taken care of, before the Thanksgiving holiday," she thought. Cherry was looking forward to Thanksgiving and some rest and fun.

Cherry approached the new, four-story, concrete building with interest. It was big, since it served an enormous area. Gwen had said it encompassed her nursing district too, and Bertha and Josie's districts as well.

As Cherry went up the steps, crowds of children and young people streamed out, on their way home to supper. They were talking animatedly, making dates to meet here tomorrow. Cherry went into the entrance hall and found the receptionist.

"I'm Nurse Ames, visiting nurse for District Four. I'd like to talk with someone here about two of my patients." Her uniform was her badge.

"Certainly, nurse. I'll ask one of our social workers to see you."

While the receptionist telephoned upstairs, Cherry looked in at one of the rooms. It was a studio, littered with colored dishes still wet from the pottery wheel, a half-finished portrait in clay, vases in the making. A woman in a smock was helping two young girls put away their tools. The clay and pigments smelled cool and pungent.

"Interesting?" laughed a voice at Cherry's shoulder.

She turned to find a pleasant young woman in a pretty, red sports dress. "It certainly is interesting! Wish I had time to join that class. Is there a fee?"

"There is no fee for any activity in a community house. Everyone is welcome. We are supported by contributions. Oh, I might tell you my name, mightn't I?

I'm Evelyn Stanley and you're Miss Ames, aren't you? We're always glad to have visitors, and especially the visiting nurses."

"How do you do, Miss Stanley. I've been wanting for a long time to get here. I've never been through a settlement house."

"Then I shall take you on a tour! The entire community is proud of Laurel House—"

Starting here on the semibasement floor, the social worker showed Cherry various rooms: the clay-working studio, the art studio with its easels and drawing boards and charcoal dust, a weaving room full of looms and bright yarns, a jewelry-making shop, a leather workroom, a sewing room with machines, a big metal and carpentry shop.

"This is our Craft School," Miss Stanley said. "I think a community house would be welcome in any neighborhood, but it's a necessity here where families can't afford to give their children normal outlets. Without Laurel House, our boys and girls would be loafing on street corners and getting into trouble. Some of the so-called 'bad ones' have turned into our very best and most enthusiastic members."

Beyond, on this street-level floor, Cherry saw a small auditorium with a generous stage, orchestra pit, and balconies.

"We give plays and concerts here, with neighborhood talent. We put on good shows, too! One of our girls is now a featured player in the movies, two of our boys now have their own dance bands, and—you'd better stop me, Miss Ames! We have a big gymnasium, besides, for sports and dances and parties. Always something going on."

They went upstairs. Here they paused at pleasant sitting rooms for neighbors' gatherings—"or for lectures and informal classes," said Miss Stanley. "We have over two thousand adults coming here faithfully at night to improve their English, and study American history and civics. Many of them have been well educated in other languages."

Up another flight, the social worker led Cherry into a room crowded helter-skelter with everything from dressers, tools, books, to egg beaters, overalls, and even a spinning wheel.

"This is our Swap Shop," Evelyn Stanley explained. "If a family hasn't the money to buy something they need or want, they can come here and trade in something they do have. Every article is priced by an impartial appraiser, but no money is exchanged."

Cherry thought this an eminently practical and direct system. Her eye fell on a sewing basket which Bertha Larsen would certainly like to own.

"How would I buy that, Miss Stanley?"

"You'd have to bring in some article in exchange."

"Suppose my article was valued at—oh, a dollar more than this sewing kit?"

"Then you'd get a dollar's credit."

On the third floor were still more cheerful rooms. "For group work and recreation, Miss Ames. Across the hall we run our Nursery School." The social worker held open a door and Cherry saw playpens, shelves of toys, charts on the wall describing a child's growth, diets, medical and dental care. "On the top floor is our Health Department. We're hoping to open a Music School too, someday, if we can build around the corner."

Cherry was impressed. Her civic consciousness was having a lively awakening. She thanked Evelyn Stanley for the tour.

As they went down the stairs again, Cherry talked to the social worker about Miss Culver and Gustave Persson, describing their problems.

"Indeed we can help them," Miss Stanley said. "We're obliged to you for letting us know of people who need help. For Mr. Persson, give him this—" She took from her pocket a card marked: Laurel House, wrote in Uncle Gustave's name, and under it, Carpentry and Construction. This meant, she said, that he was invited to come here to the Craft Shop and build to his heart's content with Laurel House tools and materials.

"Thank you! He'll probably want to build you that new Music School," Cherry laughed.

Miss Stanley's eyes sparkled. "Maybe we'll let him! Practically every person who comes here ends up giving Laurel House more than it gave him."

"And about Miss Culver? She's not well enough to walk this far and I think, too, that being among so many—well, noisy children would wear her out. She's still convalescent."

The social worker nodded. "We could send her something to do at home. Have you any idea what she'd enjoy?"

Cherry thought of those windows looking down on the street, and what Miss Culver had said about the silvery light. That mended upholstery too, like a fine piece of embroidery—Miss Culver's hands must be as deft as her eyes were responsive. Then Cherry thought of the art room with its easels.

"What about paints and drawing paper, Miss Stanley? Maybe Miss Culver would like to try painting what she sees from her window. Or does she need instruction?"

"Some of the finest artists never had instruction. If your Miss Culver has a smidgeon of talent, it will come out by itself. If not—well, almost everyone enjoys messing around with colors."

So it was arranged that Cherry would return in a few days and pick up paints, brushes, a big pad of water-color paper, folding easel—everything Miss Culver would need. She again thanked the social worker and left Laurel House.

On the sidewalk Cherry paused to shake her curly head at its hospitably open door. "There may not be a

Santa Claus, but there certainly are some goodhearted, generous people in this world!"

It was night now, six-thirty—as usual, Cherry was hopelessly late in leaving her district. She ran for the bus. Hopping on, she was appalled to see that she would have to ride with that awful driver, Smith. Gingerly she handed him a dime and shrank back while he gave her change.

"Step back inna bus, back inna bus," he growled at her.

Cherry stepped back, decidedly not wanting an argument. Just as the traffic lights started to change, a hurrying woman hopped on the bus step. It was Ingrid Persson. The driver all but slammed the door on her hand.

"In or out, lady—make up yer mind!"

Mrs. Persson was so startled that she could not move for a second. Then she fumbled for her fare.

"Ya made me miss the light! Now aintcha gonna pay yer fare?"

The whole bus was listening. Mrs. Persson flushed with humiliation. Her hands trembled as she futilely searched her purse. Cherry felt almost as badly as Mrs. Persson did. She was angry, besides, with the bullying driver. With a hello to Mrs. Persson, she put a nickel in the box for her, and hoped that would smooth the incident over.

But the driver sneered. Mrs. Persson looked about to cry. Cherry did something she would never have done had she not been in uniform and in her own district. She turned to the bus driver and said quietly:

"Now look, driver, that's enough."

He roared. "Smart nurse, huh? Mind yer own business!

"This neighborhood is my official business. Even you are my business." Cherry did not raise her voice, but she knew it carried all over the bus. "Smith, what makes you so nasty that everybody hates you?"

"Let 'em hate me! Who cares?" But he did care. He had turned red.

"Don't you know you're making yourself a laughingstock?" That hit home, too. "Why don't you try being—not pleasant—just silent, Driver Smith?"

Then Cherry turned away and sat down, shaking and surprised at this unaccustomed thing she had done. Mrs. Persson had taken a seat away out of sight in the back of the bus.

There was not another word out of the driver. Even when a fat lady puffed up the bus step and made him miss a green light, Driver Smith did not yell. He still glared, but his new-found silence was remarkable.

Cherry, with the rest of the inquisitive passengers, was so astonished that she rode along with her eyes glued on Driver Smith. Barely in time did she notice the bus stopping where she could distantly see the Gregory mansion.

Cherry pressed her face close to the window and peered down the shadowy blocks, straining to see the outlines of the house. A single, faint light glimmered there. Dark, bare trees rose in a protective thicket around the mansion and concealed an eighteen-year-old mystery.

CHAPTER VIII

Parties and Clues

JOSIE FRANKLIN HAD A BEAU. HE WAS A YOUNG DOCTOR she had met through her work and his name was John Brent. Young as the girls themselves, he was easygoing enough to be amused rather than ruffled by Josie's rattlebrained remarks. In fact, not even a houseful of girls could ruffle Dr. Johnny. He would sit peacefully on their living-room sofa, chuckling at Josie's *non sequiturs*, and ducking the scramble of six nurses with no more protest than a grin. Or if Dr. Johnny took Josie to the movies, he comfortably invited the whole Spencer Club too. Dr. John Brent was showing up at the apartment more and more frequently.

"Josie has a beau, Josie has a beau," Gwen chanted. It was Sunday noon, and the girls were loafing over a combination breakfast-lunch. "Well, it's about time one of us had a nice new romance."

"It isn't a romance and Johnny isn't a beau." Josie blinked behind her glasses. "He just likes me. Some. That's all."

"Oh," said Vivian. "I suppose Dr. Johnny sits on our sofa because he can't think of anything better to do? He comes around to call on the entire Spencer Club?"

"He likes our peppermints and our pretty wallpaper." Cherry grinned. "He doesn't like Josie, oh, no."

Josie wrinkled her forehead and turned to quiet little Mai Lee for help.

"Is he really a beau, Mai Lee?"

Mai Lee smiled. "I think Johnny likes you better than you realize."

Josie wonderingly set down her cup. "Well, what do you know! But honestly, I think he has fun with the whole gang of us."

Bertha returned with a fresh pot of coffee. "I miss *my* John. He keeps writing that I should come back to the farm and marry him, that we've been waiting long enough." Bertha's china-blue eyes had a faraway look. It was one of the rare times that Bertha spoke of her fiancé, with whom she had grown up.

Cherry, winding one black curl around her finger, wondered about her own romance department. It was conspicuous by its absence. Wade Cooper was a highly satisfactory young man, but he was out of the Air Forces now and back home in Tucson, hard at work starting a business. And there simply was no one else at the moment.

Cherry looked around speculatively at the other girls. Gwen knew someone she liked but he was in St. Louis. Mai Lee and Vivian were as lacking in dates, here in New York, as Cherry was.

"Hey, kids. You know what?" Cherry said slowly. "I just thought about this for the first time—We've all been so busy with our work that I guess we haven't done any thinking at all."

"Thinking about what?" Cherry's serious tone caught their attention.

"Just this. That except for Josie, we haven't any beaux or callers or friends. That—darn it!—we're all wrapped up in ourselves and our work. We never see anyone socially but one another." She shook back her dark curls. "I've just waked up to the awful truth. We're getting—uh—"

"Narrow," Mai Lee supplied. "Insular."

Vivian nodded. "Yes, we are. Here we have the apartment fixed up, and we haven't given a single party."

Gwen snapped her fingers. "I knew there was something I meant to do. Look up the Taylor family. They used to live in our town and last year they moved to New York. I went all through school with Ben Taylor."

Cherry suddenly remembered a Hilton family, the Coreys, living now in New York.

"Why, we know lots of people if we'd only come out of our shells!"

Bertha Larsen, like Vivian, had no contacts in New York. But she suggested it was easy to get acquainted through the various States' clubs, or the Ys, or the Spencer Nursing School Alumni Association.

"We could invite 'em all to come see our blue furniture!" Josie piped up. "Johnny thinks it's quite a sight," she added ambiguously.

"All right," the Spencer Club voted, "we'll look up these people and we *will* invite 'em."

Cherry's Corey family turned out to consist of an aged couple, plus a nephew aged fifty. The younger members of the Corey family, whom Cherry remembered, had gone to live in California. Cherry called on these elderly people with some disappointment, but politely asked them to come to tea. To her amazement, the old couple amiably traveled all the way down to the Village one Sunday afternoon, for the tea party. The girls invited Mr. and Mrs. Jenkins from upstairs, too, and asked Dr. Johnny to bring another young man with him. With six guests and six girls, the afternoon was a more pleasant one than Cherry had hoped for. Old Mr. and Mrs. Corey's enjoyment was a reward in itself. And as Vivian said afterwards, "I don't see why all our friends must be our own age. It's comfortable to know older people!"

Gwen's Taylor family, she announced delightedly after a long telephone conversation, was intact. Mrs. Taylor had asked Gwen to dinner, and Ben, the youngest son, would be coming down to see them some evening soon.

"I couldn't ever think of Ben Taylor as a romance," Gwen told the others. "Not after he dipped my pigtails in desk inkwells at school, for years and years. Yep, I wore pigtails in my youth. But Ben's an awfully nice fellow. You'll see."

Ben came by one Friday evening. He was a lanky, sandy-haired, nice-looking young man, easy to talk to. He got along famously with the Spencer Club and with quiet Dr. Johnny who came in, too—Josie's beau was "practically a fixture by now," Cherry said. Ben was intrigued by the blue furniture and its history, devoured large amounts of refreshments, and asked if he could come back with some of his pals—to see the blue furniture. Like Johnny Brent, Ben doubted that such furniture actually existed.

"Yes, I see it with my own eyes," he admitted, "but, of course, it's just a mirage. It's not bad-looking," Ben added courteously. "Just amazing."

They set a date and a few evenings later Ben showed up with three more young men. They all carried assorted paper boxes and bags.

"Refreshments," Ben said gallantly. "Also, Dan, Tiny

(because he isn't), and George, in that order. George's real name is Clarence, but we never tell anyone that."

George indignantly denied the whole thing and grinned at Vivian in particular. Tiny was a very big, outdoor fellow who laughed heartily when he looked out on what they called their "garden." Danny had an infectious smile and feet that kept breaking into tap steps. Like lanky, loose-jointed Ben, Danny was eager to turn on the radio and dance. Dr. Johnny just sat relaxed on the couch looking amused, as usual.

"But first we have to inspect the blue furniture," Ben announced. They all trooped down the hall. "Gentlemen, I submit that these blue objects are distinctive, unique, the only ones of their kind in the world."

Tiny sat down on one of the blue chairs, trying it. It creaked under his weight. Mai Lee hastily asked him if he wouldn't help her unpack the refreshments, for which the surprised hostesses offered thanks. Tiny then made the mistake of trying to squeeze into the kitchenette, and they heard pots and pans clattering down.

"I guess we'd better dance, at that," Cherry said and turned on the radio.

They danced for half an hour, until they were breathless. Even Dr. Johnny, who preferred to "just sit," was pressed into service as a partner. Finally, when they could find no more dance music on the radio, they sat down around the living room to talk.

George wanted to play games. Apparently he knew dozens of them, and started off with riddles.

"How do you make slow horses fast?"

"Say giddap," Josie solemnly guessed.

"Spurs. Sugar," Cherry and Danny called out.

"Nope. To make slow horses fast, don't feed 'em." The others objected. "A pun!"

"All right, no puns," George agreed. "Why is it useless to send a telegram to Washington today?"

They all thought. Dr. Johnny murmured, "Because Washington is dead."

"Right! Hmm, a sharpie," George approved. "Which is bigger, Mr. Bigger or his baby?"

"That's silly," sniffed Bertha Larsen.

"The baby is just a little Bigger," said George. "Stop laughing—here's a different kind. Will someone give me a piece of paper?"

Vivian handed him the telephone pad. George wrote down, and asked them to read:

F U N E X?
S, V F X.
F U N E M?
S, V F M.
O K, M N X.

They sputtered and puzzled, and finally it dawned on them. They declaimed triumphantly, "Have you any eggs? Yes, we have eggs. Have you any ham? Yes, we have ham. Okay, ham and eggs." This talk made Tiny look hungry.

Dr. Johnny had a game in which "It" must not laugh or smile. Since Tiny was mumbling, far too soon, about refreshments, the embarrassed boys chose him to be "It." The young doctor explained that the object of the game was to make "It" laugh or smile against his will, by asking foolish questions. "It" had to give ridiculous answers. "Everyone but Tiny can laugh all he wants. All right, go!"

Tiny stood up and faced the crowd, his expression deadpan.

Ben asked dramatically, "Why do you pour glue in your pockets all the time?"

"So I'll stick at things." They chuckled. Tiny assumed a scowl.

"How recently have you telephoned an elephant?" Gwen threw at him.

"Last week, but Jumbo's trunk line was out of order." Tiny very nearly smiled at his own joke. They were laughing by now.

Mai Lee inquired, "Have you ever dug for clams in a mining camp?"

That was too ridiculous for Tiny. He broke down and guffawed. "Hasta la Coca-Cola" Tiny gave up. "Who's 'It' next?"

This nonsense went on and on until it suddenly was ten o'clock. Tiny said in so many words that he was starved.

The girls again told their guests how extra nice they were to bring refreshments and excitedly opened the packages. They found man-sized sandwiches and cakes, to which they added glasses of milk and a big bowl of apples.

Having supper quieted them down. The talk turned to New York, since the city was new to the girls, and then to their districts. Mai Lee described Chinatown and Vivian enthused about Long Island. In the midst of this rather perfunctory conversation, Cherry dropped a bombshell.

"Did I ever tell you about the mysterious recluse in my district? The woman no one has seen for eighteen years?"

"Your mysterious wha-a-at?"

"Eighteen years! Why did she do it?"

Immediately everybody's mood changed. Cherry herself, sitting on one of the blue chairs, looked sober.

"No one seems to know why she did it. But it looks as if she intends to stay locked in that mysterious old house until the day she dies."

The young men asked practical questions: how did she manage to live? Cherry explained about the arrangements with the grocer, the furnace man, the well-dressed man who apparently was a banker or lawyer and who came once a year. Even Dr. Johnny was affected by the story. The girls wanted to know what Mary Gregory was like.

"Nobody really knows what she is like," Cherry replied. "The grocer saw her only once, eighteen years ago, and he gives a good report on her. But the rest of the neighborhood believes—Well, there is a disturbing legend about her."

Cherry broke off, debating whether to repeat what struck her as fantastic. But the others insisted that she go on.

"Well, just this afternoon," Cherry began hesitantly, "I was walking past that old Victorian mansion, but on the other side of the street. I started to cross the street when two children called out to me, 'Don't go over there! Stay away from the witch's house!'" She smiled. "A little boy of eight, and a cute little girl about five. They were protecting me, you understand. They told me the same tale I'd heard from a soda fountain boy—a boy who grew up in that neighborhood—"

Cherry repeated Joe Baxter's tale of the strange shadows at Mary Gregory's windows at night. She described the thing that Joe said looked like hangman's gallows and the eerie figure flitting around it.

"Whew! That is odd," Ben Taylor admitted.

"Are you sure," Mai Lee asked, "that it isn't something the children have merely imagined they saw, or made up out of whole cloth?"

Cherry shook her head. "Some of the grownups have seen the same scary performance with their own eyes."

There was a hush.

"Maybe she was performing some curious rites of her own," Dr. Johnny mused.

Cherry sighed. "If there is something strange in that house, as the legend says, Mary Gregory keeps it well hidden."

"Why only at night?" two of the guys asked curiously.

"Because witches appear only at night," Josie said in all seriousness.

They smiled at that. Yet the testimony of a whole neighborhood was not to be ignored. Dr. Johnny asked if anyone ever saw the woman.

Again Cherry hesitated. It sounded so incredible, dreamlike, to say it aloud.

"One of my patients, a Mrs. Persson, used to see Mary Gregory summer nights, late, on an upstairs balcony. Just a glimpse of a white dress, and a white, ghostly figure. Sometimes, she says, you could hear piano music coming from that house long past midnight."

"Why doesn't someone just go up to the front door and ring the bell?" Josie inquired.

"Neighborhood people have tried that," Cherry said. "Mary Gregory never answers. But I talked to—"

Cherry shook her head, troubled, wondering why she was telling all this. It had frozen their cheerful little party into a kind of horror. Perhaps she was talking about it because it was weighing on her mind.

"You talked to whom?" the others prodded.

Cherry lifted her dark eyes. "To the furnace man and the postman. The postman didn't reveal much. He did tell me she sends and receives mail, but it—wait, you're guessing wrong! The mail is mostly to department stores and a coal company and a bank and so forth, to enable her to order things she needs, without stirring out of her house. You see? Beyond that, I suspect the postman is as mystified as I am."

"And the furnace man?"

"Just notes to and from her, about coal and repairs. The furnace man never once has seen her. Doesn't even hear her moving around. He says it's uncanny and that something unearthly is going on in that old house."

It was strange, very strange, they all muttered. What they could not understand, above all, was the gallows and the grimly dancing figure silhouetted on the blinds at night. Cherry was forced to believe that although the "witch" legend was superstition, Mary Gregory really did do something peculiar behind drawn blinds at night.

CHAPTER IX

Unknown Neighbors

THE LONG, COLD, FALL RAINS HAD STARTED. THE TREES stood bare now on Cherry's district, lashed by heavy winds. Bundled into her heavy overcoat and overshoes, Cherry tramped the quiet streets, going from patient to patient. Sometimes it was lonely, out alone in the pouring rain day after day, entering strangers' homes and working hard to make friends of them, stopping for lunch at any counter or diner that was near.

Today, at least, she was going to see a family she already knew, the Perssons. Cherry started off, black bag swinging, to check up on Uncle Gustave. The card of invitation to the Craft Shop still was tucked in her purse: there had been so many urgent sick calls recently that this had had to wait.

"I could walk to the Perssons' by passing Miss Gregory's house. It's only a little out of my way."

The Victorian mansion loomed up in the pouring rain. Because its protective trees were stripped of leaves now, Cherry could see the house more clearly. The windows were richly curtained in lace, in an old-fashioned style. They all seemed to be tightly closed. The heavy, oak door on the porch had swollen from the rain: it might be almost impossible to pry open. Probably it had not been opened in years. Cherry went along the fence to the back of the house, and peered at the back steps.

"Wish I could just go inside the kitchen and call out to ask if she's all right," she thought. Yet she had no right of entry. Mary Gregory had not summoned the nurse. Still—

Impulsively Cherry unlatched the gate and walked across the wet back yard. She was surprised at how hard her heart started to beat. She mounted the steps and raised her fist to knock. But some curious respect for the recluse restrained her. Or was it pity? Whatever it was, Cherry slowly withdrew her hand, turned, and went away.

It was a long walk to the Perssons'. Cherry got thoroughly drenched.

When Ingrid Persson opened the door and saw the dripping nurse, she exclaimed: "I will make you hot coffee!"

Cherry giggled. "Do I look that drowned? How are you, Mrs. Persson? No coffee, really, thanks."

Both of them avoided mentioning the incident of the bus and Driver Smith. Mrs. Persson led Cherry in to see Uncle Gustave.

"Another nosebleed yesterday, Miss Ames."

"What he needs," Cherry said softly, "is not medicine but psychology."

They came into his orderly room. The little man sat up weakly on his bed. He was fully dressed but downcast, his beloved tools untouched.

Cherry checked him over, asked a few questions, then came to the real point of her visit.

"How would you like to build as much as you like, with all the tools and materials supplied to you?"

His eyes turned bluer than ever with delight. Then he scoffed, "There is no such chance."

"But there is! Laurel House—"

"No. Charity I do not take."

"This isn't charity. You join and become a member." Cherry carefully explained. Hope crept back into Uncle Gustave's pinched face. "And here is the membership card Miss Stanley sent you."

Mrs. Persson beamed with approval. The little man reached for the card, then let his hand fall limp. "Now I remember. Constant told me. It is for children. For learners. To learn to hammer nails. Bah! I am no child, I am a master craftsman."

Cherry had not foreseen this valid objection. "Maybe—maybe you could become an instructor," she groped, and hoped that she was not encroaching on Miss Stanley's jurisdiction. "Or—ah—Laurel House wants to build a Music School. They need help, advice, an experienced builder. I told them about you and they wish you would help."

"Go once," Mrs. Persson urged. "Only once, Uncle Gustave. See how it is."

Uncle Gustave was sitting up straight now. "If they need me, yes. Yes, I will go and help them."

Cherry and Ingrid Persson exchanged grins. Cherry left some vitamin tablets, but she did not think Uncle Gustave would need them now.

"Will you stay for coffee and *kondis*, Miss Ames?"

Cherry hesitated. She did not like to refuse this woman who was so starved for friends. But work pressed her, Cherry regretfully explained, and she took her leave.

Her calls led her again past the lonely old mansion. Cherry stood for a moment beside the fence, wondering about Mary Gregory, wondering what that house held. Perhaps she would never find out.

"This isn't getting my calls made!" Determinedly Cherry started out again on her round of healing.

But Cherry could not stop speculating about the mysterious recluse, even though some colorful people filled her afternoon. The Sergeyevskys were among today's patients, with their high-necked blouses, tea, and strangled English. Cherry called on a couple who kept twelve cats. She found a woman living in a damp cellar, and coughing, and promised to help find more healthful quarters.

She showed a nervous young father how to bathe his brand-new baby: the baby stood the ordeal better than the young man. Cherry went back to the Terrell cottage, where Jimmy was all but well now, and gave weary little Mrs. Terrell final instructions on cleaning up after the contagious illness.

All these people seemed so lonesome. They were so glad to have a visitor. And Cherry was touched by the respect and affection her uniform called forth.

Miss Culver was last on today's list, because Cherry had to go to the settlement house and pick up the painting kit for her. Cherry wished she could be doing something for Mary Gregory, too. That woman must be far lonelier than all the rest.

Laurel House was full of lights and people and activity. It was a cheering, sociable place to come to on a rainy day. Cherry asked for the social worker, Evelyn Stanley, and waited, peering in at the pottery studio meanwhile.

"Hello, Miss Ames! The painting set is all ready." Miss Stanley came running lightly down the stairs. Today she wore emerald green, and looked as thoroughly alive as Laurel House itself. "Why, Miss Ames. What are you looking so pensive about?"

Cherry pushed her curls off her red cheeks. "Ohhh—maybe it's the rain, Miss Stanley. Or maybe it's because I've been seeing so many lonesome people today. You know, I come from the Middle West where everybody knows everybody else. If you don't know 'em, you say hello anyway and pretty soon you get acquainted. I just can't understand it, here in the city, where neighbors live side by side and don't have a real friend outside of their own families."

"I know. It worries me, too," Evelyn Stanley said. "And a settlement house simply can't reach everyone. Big cities are lonely."

"I worry about lonesome people like my Perssons and my Miss Culver." And Mary Gregory, Cherry added silently.

"Me, too," the social worker said. "I wake up at night sometimes, wondering who's all alone, only a few blocks away."

"The pity of it is, they'd like one another if only they could get acquainted."

The two young women sat down on a bench together, brooding.

"I did have a piece of an idea," Cherry said cautiously.

Miss Stanley brightly glanced up. "Mm? Let's hear it."

"You don't know about me and my ideas," Cherry warned.

"Oh, you too? I'm another dangerous idea woman."

They laughed and liked each other. Cherry said:

"Well, it's this. Everybody's interested in good things to eat. No matter how little people may have in common, even if they came originally from different countries, they'd enjoy sampling one another's cooking. They'd have food to talk about, for a start. Maybe if we had—oh, call it neighbors' dinners—people could get acquainted that way."

Evelyn Stanley's eyes had an absorbed, glazed look which Cherry suspected spelled action. "You have something there! Matter of fact, I think it was tried in another section of New York City, and people ended up being friends. They went into one another's homes—it's nicest at home—each family took a turn playing host—"

"I'm afraid people around here haven't the means or facilities," Cherry said. "Is there any chance that Laurel House could lend a hand? I'm sure lots of my people would like to be invited—bring their pet foods as the price of admission—" She could ask Josie and Bertha and Gwen, whose districts adjoined and were served by Laurel House, to invite their patients too.

"—and invite not only your patients. Everybody! Dishes of all nationalities, all regions," Evelyn Stanley was planning aloud. "I'll ask our head caseworker right away."

The two of them looked at each other like conspirators.

"We're nearly forgetting Miss Culver's paints!"

Cherry's head was full of all these possible doings when she trotted back through her district, went upstairs, and knocked on Miss Culver's door.

"Who is it?"

"It's the nurse, Miss Culver—with a surprise for you!"

The door opened onto the gracious, shabby room and some of the weariness went out of Miss Culver's face. "Something for me?"

"Open it and tell me if you like it," Cherry said eagerly. "If you don't, we'll figure out something else—"

Miss Culver's hands shook as she undid the big, bulky package. Cherry suspected it was a long time since anyone had given this gentle lady a present.

"Why—why, it's paints!" Miss Culver shyly fingered the brushes, the bottles of pigment. "But, my dear Miss Ames, this will be wasted on me. Hadn't you better give it to someone who can paint?"

"How do you know you can't paint?" Cherry demanded, smiling at her.

A slow smile lit up Miss Culver's face. "Do you know, I've wondered if I couldn't paint—a little. I've sat here at my window and wished I could try—Oh, I'm going to enjoy this. Thank you very much indeed, Miss Ames."

Cherry explained that the gift came from Laurel House, and that Miss Culver, when she grew stronger, would be welcome in their painting group. She showed Miss Culver how the easel opened, and stood it at the window, adjusted low so that the frail woman could paint sitting down.

Then Cherry attempted to check Miss Culver's physical condition, but that lady was thinking too hard about her painting kit for Cherry to get any but sketchy answers. However, Cherry was satisfied with her improvement. She chuckled at Miss Culver's parting comment:

"Twelve hours to wait for daylight. Or possibly I could paint at night—tonight—"

Cherry said good night and caught the bus, to go home.

Instantly her attention was riveted, for the driver was Driver Smith. And he did not yell, snarl, or glower at Cherry as she climbed aboard and handed him her fare.

"Hello," she said tentatively.

"Hmph!" He stiffly handed her change.

Twin devils danced in Cherry's dark eyes. "Can you tell me, please, if the Junction Avenue entrance to the subway is open at this hour?" This was not Driver Smith's business, just general information. But Cherry itched to know if he would say, as usual: "Whyncha get off there and see?"

He said: "Yeah."

Cherry was careful to respond, "Thanks a lot." He looked incredulous, then embarrassed.

Cherry went back in the bus and sat down. Triumph! Driver Smith had actually been accommodating. Crossly, grudgingly, yes. But her needling him last time had helped. She sat there giggling to herself and wondering if his temper might further improve. Maybe if she nudged him every now and then—

The bus pulled, not yanked, to a stop at Mary Gregory's street. As usual, Cherry pressed her face against the window and peered out. But the rain and the dark were too dense for her to see anything beyond street lights and puddles.

An hour later, Cherry tramped into the apartment, tired, hungry, soggy. A note was propped on the mantel, against Ann's clock:

"Too gosh-darn tired to cook. Come one, come all to the Witch's Cave. (signed) Bertha, Vivian, Mai Lee."

That was their name for an orange-painted basement restaurant where their neighbors, Mr. and Mrs. Jenkins, often dined. The couple was there again tonight, and smiled at Cherry as she made her way to the girls' table for six in a corner.

"You're the last one in, Cherry," they greeted her.

"I'm done in," she groaned. "Have you kids eaten up everything in the Witch's larder?"

"What keeps you so late on your district, anyhow?"

Cherry made a face at them. "Oh, making plans at Laurel House."

"For what? We want in on this, too!"

Cherry turned away for a moment to order her meal. Then she repeated to the other nurses her conversation with Evelyn Stanley. Their faces glowed as the idea, of lonesome neighbors getting acquainted, caught on. Bedlam reigned at their table as various versions of dinners, festivals, and parties were sifted. Finally they agreed that—all factors considered—a Christmas party at Laurel House, for the entire area, would be the best choice.

"That is, if the head worker agrees. They probably have some sort of Christmas party, anyway."

"But this one is going to be superspecial!"

Mai Lee said wistfully, "Vivi and I *would* have to be assigned miles away. But we'll help you, won't we, Vivi?"

In the midst of all this enthusiasm, Cherry retired into her thoughts.

"What's on the Ames mind?" Gwen asked. "The mysterious recluse in your district?"

"Don't joke, Gwen," Vivian said. "It's not funny. Poor creature!"

"Have you learned any more about her?" they all asked.

Cherry rose from the table. "No. I wish I could find out, and help her. I can't stop thinking about her."

CHAPTER X

In Hiding

IT WAS A RELIEF TODAY TO COME OFF THE RAINY DISTRICT streets, and into the Jonas delicatessen. It was warm and spicy-smelling in here, and Cherry was scolded, fussed over, and bountifully fed. She thawed out and relaxed.

She was busy discovering that her frost-nipped ears still were attached to her head, when she noticed Mr. Jonas's expression. The old man was fidgeting with a calendar, and frowning and shaking his head.

"Anything wrong, Mr. Jonas?"

He glanced up, and his absent-minded blue eyes were cloudy. "Maybe so, maybe not. It is only a little thing. But I do not like it."

"Something wrong in the neighborhood?" Cherry asked with quick concern. This district was hers, intimately hers by now.

"Papa!" Mrs. Jonas called. "You forgot to order tomorrow's milk and cream! You think the cows should remember?"

He called back wearily to his wife, "How should I think of milk and cream when that poor, lonely woman is maybe in trouble?"

"What poor, lonely woman?" Cherry pricked up her ears. "Mary Gregory?"

"Yes, yes, Mary Gregory. Only a little thing but"—Mr. Jonas riffled again through the leaves of the calendar—"never before has it happened. Never once in eighteen years!"

Cherry stopped eating and stared. "Tell me!"

Mr. Jonas shrugged. "All right, you are the nurse, you are a good girl, I can tell you. But do not tell the neighborhood or they will come in crowds around her house. She would be terrified. Well—" He paused and stared into space.

"Well, darling. This morning I sent my delivery boy over to Miss Gregory's house to get her basket and the order for her week's supply of food. For the first time in eighteen years, *ever*, there is no basket, no check, no note. No nothing. This is not like her, she is clockwork. So I am worried. I send the boy back three hours later to see if she has only been a little delayed with the order. He comes back, just before you come in here for your lunch, and he tells me he found nothing."

"Papa! What does the little nurse think?"

"The little nurse thinks," Cherry said, struggling into her overshoes and coat, "that she had better find Officer O'Brien and talk to him."

"Good, good." Mr. Jonas nodded his head. He consulted his old-fashioned pocket watch. "At this hour he should be reporting back at the station house. But hurry, he goes out in his patrol car again."

Out in the icy rain Cherry walked as fast as she could the several blocks to the police station. She was just in time to catch Officer O'Brien.

The policeman was a powerful, rosy-faced man, solid as an oak tree in his blue uniform. He and Cherry had met earlier, when the children of the neighborhood brought him word of a great event—a new nurse had come! He smiled at her broadly and held out a tremendous hand.

"Well, now, Miss Ames!" he boomed. "What brings you here on this wet day?"

Cherry grinned back at him, wondering if she would ever learn one-tenth of the shrewd and kindly insight into human nature which showed in Officer O'Brien's bright glance. She had heard about him—as quick and fearless with a thug as he was patient and merry with a lost child.

"Officer O'Brien, Mr. Jonas told me that Mary Gregory—"

"Ah, so you're troubled about her, too?"

"If she's sick—or had an accident in there—" Cherry repeated what Mr. Jonas had told her. "I don't want to break in on her privacy, but still—"

"Nurse, I'll tell you a bit of a secret. I make it my business to pass her house daily. Often's the time I step to the door and shout: 'Are you all right? Do you want for anything?' I never see Mary Gregory but she calls back: 'Thank you, I'm all right.' Once I let a doctor in, years ago."

Cherry felt better. "Do you plan to go in now?"

The big policeman nodded. "After what you've just told me, yes, ma'am! This very minute, in fact. This may be an emergency, we don't know. I want you to go in with me, nurse."

They left the station house together and got into the patrol car. It was a brief drive to the mansion.

Cherry tingled all the way over. Now, suddenly, she was actually to see this mysterious woman! The urge to talk to the woman who had unhealthily hidden herself away pricked Cherry's nursing instinct. Not medicine but psychology . . . Officer O'Brien, driving, was silent, thinking hard.

At the Gregory house they parked and Cherry followed Officer O'Brien out of the police car. To her surprise, she walked laggingly, along the fence toward the back gate. She felt almost numb. Curious and concerned as she was about the recluse, still Cherry felt reluctant at what she had to do. As if she were prying into a secret not meant for her to know. Or as if she might have to gaze upon some unutterable tragedy she would rather not witness.

"This isn't like me, or like any good nurse," Cherry remonstrated with herself. "It's odd. I guess I'm afraid. Yes, actually afraid of what I may find in there."

Officer O'Brien, ahead of her, was moving slowly too. He, too, admitted that he had no liking for this delicate, unpredictable task. They stood talking outside the silent mansion, the nurse and the big policeman.

"I'll escort you in, nurse. Legal right of entry, and so forth. Besides, you never know what these queer birds may do. I sort of remember her father had an old gun collection in the house. She might get panicky."

Cherry said stoutly, "From the orderly way she lives, I'm pretty certain she's sane. I don't think we have to be afraid of any violence. If anyone's going to be frightened and at bay, it will be Mary Gregory."

She tried to imagine how this strange woman would feel to have her long seclusion invaded by strangers. Officer O'Brien seemed to be pondering and worrying over the same thing. He and Cherry looked unhappily at each other. This was like hunting down a helpless creature. At length she said:

"You know, I think it might be better if you stayed downstairs and let me go up to see her alone. Then if I need you, I can call you."

"I expect so, ma'am. Guess a woman could handle this more tactful than a cop." He seemed rather relieved to have it settled that way.

He unlatched the back gate. The front door had not been opened in years, he explained. With a skeleton key fitted into its lock, the back door swung open easily. Cherry followed the broad, blue-coated figure in.

They were standing in a kitchen, immaculate, up-to-date, except that beside its fairly modern stove stood a very old, iron one. The house was so silent that the stillness seemed to ring.

Officer O'Brien slowly walked into the adjoining hallway and stood at the foot of the stairs. Cherry could see him glance sharply into rooms giving off the hallway, turn, open a door—apparently a cellar door—glance in. Once he stepped out of her line of vision. Instinctively she rushed a few paces forward so that she could see the policeman again, then stood rooted to the spot.

She jumped. Officer O'Brien was calling. His big voice, rather strained, echoed and re-echoed in the motionless rooms.

"Miss Gregory! Are you all right? It's the police! Are you all right?"

No answer. Not a sound. Cherry felt gooseflesh shiver down her spine.

"Are you all right? Answer me if you can!"

Only echoes replied, dying away. Officer O'Brien clumped back into the kitchen, to where Cherry stood. He wet his lips.

"Do you think she's dead?" Cherry breathed.

The policeman shook his head. "I doubt it. Doesn't add up that way." He smiled a little, grimly. "When you've pounded a beat as long as I have, you're bound to get hunches about these queer situations."

Cherry felt only dimly reassured. She was beginning to dread venturing alone through these rooms, and upstairs. It was more than ordinary dread—it was a kind of outrage to any delicacy of feeling.

"If you're ready," Officer O'Brien said, kind and gruff, reading her thoughts. "I'll wait for you at the foot of the stairs."

Cherry's gaze flew to his. He said again:

"You were right. It would be easier for *her*, to see just a young woman—a nurse—"

Cherry drew a deep breath. "All right."

"Good girl. Now suppose you take a look at the downstairs rooms first—I'm not going to barge in—"

Cherry nodded and holding tightly to the strap of her black bag, started off. Unconsciously she walked on tiptoe out into the hall. The grandfather clock out there had stopped. Its hands stood still at quarter to three.

She looked over her shoulder at Officer O'Brien. He had taken up his post at the bottom of the long, wide stairs. He waved her forward.

She entered the first of the three open doors and found herself in a high-ceilinged living room which belonged to another day. It was beautiful and faded, with satiny wallpaper, old-fashioned furniture, and thick, flowered carpet into which her steps sank without a sound. Cherry ran a finger over the surface of a gleaming table. There rose up a tiny shower of dust, the accumulation of only a day or two. Otherwise, all these inanimate things were polished, washed, waxed to the most fastidious degree.

"But the room looks dead—not lived in—" she thought, troubled. "Like a museum—no, a tomb."

In the next room, two steps down, the past had been perfectly preserved. Cherry stared at the dark oak walls, the bull's-eye windows, the black marble fireplace with roses carved into it. Here the furniture was plumply cushioned with dark-red silk, but no imprint of a living being was left. The windows were tightly closed, the heavy draperies did not stir. It was perfect, immaculate, and dead.

Cherry felt as if she were being suffocated. "It's a room for ghosts." Suddenly she saw someone staring across the room at her. She started, opened her mouth to call Officer O'Brien—It was only herself, wide-eyed. It was only her own reflection in a shadowy mirror.

"Whew! If I can scare myself, that's a new low! Go on now, Ames. Go—*on*!"

She peeked out at Officer O'Brien standing there, and smiled weakly at him, before moving on to the third room. This was a dining room, where the long-dead had dined, looking like a stage set now. A golden clock, under a Victorian glass dome, had stopped at quarter to three.

She went back into the hall.

"Find anything?"

"Nothing. I'll—I'll go upstairs."

On the broad landing she did find something.

"Hello!" she called down softly. "There are three portraits on the wall up here. A man. A woman. And a young man."

Cherry gained the second floor. Here, despite her trepidation, she sensed a different atmosphere. This upper part of the house *was* lived in. This wide upstairs hallway, with several windows, was virtually a living room. An open sewing basket lay on one of the window seats. Ivy filled a quaint plant stand. It was a relief to see and hear a small desk clock ticking away. Framing all these upstairs windows were yards and yards of meticulous hand embroidery.

"Where is she?" Cherry wondered. "Maybe she's not here at all!"

The doors to various rooms stood open. These were bedrooms: a master chamber with a faded, canopied bed, a child's room of many years ago, guest rooms furnished as Cherry vaguely remembered her grandmother's house. The beds were made, everything stood in readiness, as if for people who would never arrive.

But up at the front of the house, looking out on the street, Cherry found a sitting room. A highly personal and feminine room. Unlike the rest of the house, this apartment had quite new, informal furnishings. Besides, there was a radio, a stack of current magazines, a tray with used breakfast china on it, and a newspaper. Cherry tiptoed in and looked at the date on the newspaper. Day before yesterday.

She noticed other things. There were several letters on the desk, some opened and in various handwritings or typed, some written and ready for the mailman. One entire wall was lined with books, many of them recent. On a chair a medical book lay open at the section marked: Respiratory Disorders.

"She's been trying to treat herself," Cherry recognized. "And though part of her lives in the past, if she's in touch with the outside world, maybe there still is some hope for her."

Cherry opened the door into the other front room which gave on the street.

She caught her breath, for here Cherry found what she had been dreading.

In a vast bed rested a woman with the air of someone living in a dream. It was a haunted face, with great eyes that looked out pleadingly at Cherry.

"I—I am the neighborhood nurse," Cherry said softly.

She took a few hesitant steps toward the bed. The woman's eyes followed her. She looked frightened, as if she might cry. Cherry stopped and did not approach any nearer. The woman's hands, bare of rings, gripped the bedclothes convulsively. Around the wrists and throat of her white nightdress, and edging the sheets, was more of that hand embroidery. Her tumbled hair, against the pillow, was dark, shot with silver. The face was not young and was marked with suffering, but strangely girlish still. She reminded Cherry of some woodland animal, like a doe, injured and bewildered.

Very gently Cherry said: "If you are ill, I can treat you. But if you wish, I will go away."

The colorless lips parted. "No. Stay." Then: "Help me."

Cherry knew better than to try to make this woman talk. She was careful to talk very little herself. With the utmost gentleness, she put a thermometer between the sick woman's lips, picked up the thin wrist, counting her pulse and breathing.

"I think you have influenza, Miss Gregory. This changeable weather."

The heavy eyes lifted and asked Cherry a question.

"Yes, you should have a doctor. A nurse cannot diagnose, or prescribe treatment. Would you let me call a doctor?"

The woman turned her head on the pillow and looked away. Her great eyes searched vistas Cherry could not see: past, unhappy years, or empty years to come. Perhaps this lonely creature did not want to be cured, did not want to go on living. Sick people were often unreasoningly low in spirits.

Cherry said quickly: "You are not very ill. You will probably get well with only my help." This was true enough, but Cherry said it to drive any morbid thoughts out of the sick woman's mind. "You are going to recover, Miss Gregory. But a doctor can shorten your pain. And then, too." Cherry appealed, gambling on a motive, "it isn't quite fair to put a doctor's responsibility on a nurse's shoulders."

A sensitive glance shot from the heavy eyes. The woman faintly smiled.

"A nurse—a child, almost. Very well. A doctor."

"Thank you, Miss Gregory."

Cherry rose, excused herself and promised to be right back, then sped downstairs. Officer O'Brien was still where she had left him. He ran halfway up the stairs to meet her.

"Well? Did you find her?"

"Yes—ill, but not in any danger. Needs a doctor. Can you get one?"

"Sure, right away. I'll radio from my patrol car. Say, tell me—What's she like, hey?"

Cherry hesitated, then helplessly held out her hands. "Pathetic. Scared. And—a nice person."

"Beats me." The policeman strode off to the kitchen. "What's she scared of?"

"Life itself," Cherry murmured as he went out the back door.

Returning upstairs to the sick woman, Cherry made her comfortable, then prepared for the doctor's visit. She thought of preparing food for Mary Gregory, but did not want to feed her until after the doctor's examination.

The doctor arrived within a few minutes. It was Dr. Gray, from the near-by hospital. Cherry knew him slightly and said reassuringly to the sick woman, "This is Dr. Gray." He was middle-aged, quiet, a soothing presence, and an excellent practitioner. From the look on his face, Cherry guessed O'Brien had cautioned Dr. Gray as to the special psychological situation here.

"Hot water and towels, nurse."

"Here you are, doctor."

Like Cherry, Dr. Gray apparently had decided to talk as little as possible. It was enough of a shock to this woman to have people confront her, after her eighteen years of solitude and silence, without being subjected to a great deal of talk besides. Only the smallest and most tactful contact with her could be made at first.

"Yes, it's influenza. A mild case, fortunately. When did you last have anything to eat, Miss Gregory?"

She had to stop and think. "Yesterday."

"Nurse Ames will fix you something."

"Yes, doctor," said Cherry. She smiled to herself, thinking Mr. Jonas would be relieved to hear of this. She figured that even though Mary Gregory had gone downstairs to the kitchen yesterday, probably the rain plus her own weak condition had kept her from putting out the food basket with her check and the order.

The doctor sat thinking. "Miss Gregory, although you're not very ill, you would be more comfortable with a private nurse. Someone to take constant care of you, and cook for you. Can you—afford that? If not—"

The woman lifted a thin hand. "I—don't want that. Someone here all the time. No."

"Very well," said Dr. Gray peaceably. "The visiting nurse will be enough. Please come every day, Miss Ames, and report to me daily."

"Yes, Dr. Gray."

She glanced at Mary Gregory to see if she objected. Evidently not. Cherry rapidly figured: Must explain to Supervisor Davis so she will assign Gwen or Nurse Cornish some of my other calls, and leave me enough time for here. Will have to cook three meals for Miss Gregory on each visit. Has she a little electric stove to warm the food again? Better leave a pitcher of fruit juice beside her bed, too. Get a thermos for water. What else?

The doctor was taking his leave now. Leading Cherry into the sitting room, he gave her instructions for the patient's care. He wrote out a prescription to be filled; Cherry promised to take care of it.

Dr. Gray gazed curiously around this upstairs sitting room. "Strange, strange . . . I don't envy you, Nurse Ames, trying to learn the case history of this patient."

Cherry jumped slightly. She had not thought of this half-tragic woman as anything so impersonal as a case history. Yet, of course, Dr. Gray was right. Cherry would have to get the facts about this patient, just as with all others whom the Visiting Nurse Service served, as a matter of official procedure.

The doctor picked up his hat and bag, still thinking. "It may not do her any harm to talk—if you can ever get her started talking. In fact, it should do her good to pour out her story. And you'll have to be the one to listen," he said quietly. "Well! Have I forgotten anything?"

"I think not, doctor."

"Call me up tomorrow morning at the hospital. Oh, yes, and the policeman wants you to get in touch with him, too, for a report. Good-bye, Miss Ames. And—don't let this house unnerve you."

He left. Then Cherry heard the patrol car drive off. She was all alone now in this mansion with this strange woman.

"Nurse—" It was only a whisper.

Cherry bent over the bed. The woman extended her clenched hand, then opened it. It was a door key. To the back door, it seemed. Cherry took the key and put it into her purse. The key was still warm; it must have been under Miss Gregory's pillow.

When she turned back to the bed, the haunted eyes were closed. Asleep? Or afraid and feigning sleep? The recluse's face was wan, her expression vaporous. It was like a face half forgotten, vaguely recalled, not seen in focus, not a real and present face at all.

Cherry waited a while, until the woman's breathing grew slow and deep. Then she crept downstairs, prepared sufficient food, and brought back the laden tray. Mary Gregory was still asleep, and that was good. Cherry set the food within easy reach, adjusted windows, shades, blankets. Then, having done all she could do, she went away until the next day.

But Mary Gregory had given her the key to her house. Of her own free will. Cherry had won her trust.

CHAPTER XI

The Secret

FOR A WEEK CHERRY WENT FAITHFULLY TO THE VICtorian mansion. Every day, as she nursed and cleaned and cooked for Mary Gregory, Cherry hoped that the woman would talk. She did not talk, except to murmur words of thanks. Her wistful gaze followed Cherry at her tasks, and her first fright died away. But a trace of hostility remained.

Cherry did not press. After eighteen years alone, one did not return to the world overnight. Cherry would make occasional remarks. "It's colder out today. The children are wearing their leggings now. I met them on their way to school." Or, "Mr. Jonas says the winter squash and potatoes are coming in, if you'd like some." Or Cherry simply brought Miss Gregory the daily newspaper she found on the back step. "Did you see this article about care for the war orphans?"

Children were an appeal Miss Gregory always responded to. Once she told Cherry sadly that the neighborhood children never played in her yard any more, as they used to do.

"Oh, they talk about you often," Cherry said carefully, and smiled. "There's a fine crop of youngsters around here, isn't there?"

Mary Gregory smiled back. She closed her eyes and was silent.

This far Cherry went but no further.

She was troubled about this odd woman. What was to happen after she reached convalescence, and needed the nurse no longer? Would she slip back into her life of dreams? Cherry felt a horror at permitting that to happen again. If only she could rouse Mary Gregory—shake her into seeing that she was being afraid of mere ghosts, needlessly wasting herself.

"I won't be able to help her," Cherry realized, tramping her district these cold, December days, "until I know what those ghosts in her mind are. Until she talks to me about her past. Those three portraits—Why did she lock herself away in the first place? Why? Why?"

Knocking on doors, nursing and teaching, writing up her case records at the center, occupied only the periphery of Cherry's attention. The core of her thoughts was Mary Gregory.

The woman's affection for children—there was a clue. Children were the only people she had felt able to talk to, during any of these years. "And she regards me as a child," Cherry thought in some amusement. "As a matter of fact, *she* is the one who's not grown up—running away and refusing to face her problems." Something really crushing must have befallen her.

"She was so young, so pretty!" echoed Mr. Jonas's voice in Cherry's mind. "I was sorry for her even then."

At home at the apartment these days, Cherry was preoccupied. She scarcely heard the girls' chatter.

"The head worker at Laurel House has approved having a great, big Christmas party!"

"We'll all have to pitch in. If we could get dolls, lots of 'em, and make doll clothes, for the neighborhood children—What do you think?"

"Cherry, aren't you interested any more?"

"That's fine," Cherry said absently. "Of course I'm interested but—"

But at this moment she was concentrating on Mary Gregory. A great deal depended on Cherry's proper handling of this case. Err, and the woman would creep forever back into her shell. But with tact, insight, skill, a woman's life might be salvaged.

Cherry's supervisor at the center, Dorothy Davis, had a brisk suggestion. "Get her to move. Get her out of that mausoleum of a house, where she sees the past every day. Then she'll have to live in the present!"

"How can I get her to move?"

Supervisor and nurse held a conference, and talked the case over from every angle. Miss Davis finally admitted that, short of a fire or a Health Department order to move, Mary Gregory would probably never live elsewhere.

Cherry had learned, in this week with the recluse, that Mary Gregory was a wealthy woman. She owned the house, and had a large independent income, left her by her father. The bank handled all her affairs, and paid all her bills. Cherry thought this financial good luck, in a way, had almost spelled bad luck for Mary Gregory.

"If she'd had no funds, she would have been forced out among people, like my brave Miss Culver. She would have been a much healthier, happier, and more useful person, too. Well, maybe it isn't too late," Cherry mused. "She isn't really old, scarcely middle-aged. Half her life still stretches ahead of her. She mustn't waste that, too. If only, *only*, only she would tell me her story!"

At the Jonas delicatessen, between sips of steaming broth and bites of tangy rye bread, Cherry reported the recluse's progress. The old man, who had wondered for eighteen years as he packed up each weekly food basket and his own head grew slowly gray, remained as baffled as ever.

"To die of a broken heart, I can understand, yes. But to *half* die—to neither live nor die, it makes no sense."

Mama Jonas called from the back of the shop: "Papa! So romantical, where is the cheese?"

The old man called back indignantly, "I suppose you weren't romantical when you married me, hah?"

"Hokay, Papa, you still are my heart's blood, but if you should be so kindly—where are you putting the cheese?"

Cherry grinned and asked Mr. Jonas to help her with menus for Miss Gregory. Cooking three meals daily for her took too much time from Cherry's other patients. The grocer selected several prepared dinners to go into this week's food basket.

"Miss Gregory will be walking around soon," Cherry said. "She'll be able to get down to the kitchen and do a few light tasks. No, Mr. Jonas, there isn't anything you, or anyone, can do for her, I'm afraid."

Officer O'Brien was another interested person. When Cherry stopped by at the station house, he plied her with questions for his report, and questions out of plain, human curiosity.

"Her with her comfortable house and means, not enjoyin' life!" The big policeman shook his head. "Not even steppin' out under the blue skies! Now, mind you, Nurse Ames, I'm sorry for the poor soul but—Say, how can people be like that?"

"That's what I'm trying to figure out, too," Cherry assured him.

"Well, thanks for the report. I'll keep a weather eye on her and the house, as usual. Nobody been botherin' her? Everything all right?"

Dr. Gray, in learned language, asked the same question about Mary Gregory. Conferring softly with the nurse in the upstairs sitting room, after each visit, the doctor speculated:

"What motivated her withdrawal from life? What crisis or loss was she unable to adjust to? And what early conditioning rendered her unable or unwilling to adjust? Try to get her history, nurse."

"I am trying, Dr. Gray. But she won't break her silence."

"Keep after her. Be ingenious."

Cherry tried everything she could think of. She recalled her courses in psychology, during nursing training. She sat up late three nights studying a book on casework, which Supervisor Davis thought might help her. She challenged Miss Gregory, she coaxed her, then ignored her, offered provocative openings in conversation, struggled to rouse her sympathy or curiosity for others, offered her own sympathy to the strange woman. None of it worked. Mary Gregory merely turned away.

On the day of one of Cherry's final visits, Miss Gregory was sitting in a chair beside a window. Pale winter sunshine filtered in, illumining her face. She was almost pretty in her embroidered negligee, Cherry thought, and certainly less ghostly, more like a flesh-and-blood person now.

But she still should not be left all alone again. Cherry made a last, despairing effort.

"I'll be here again tomorrow, Miss Gregory," Cherry said, packing her black bag. "Then after that I won't come any more, unless you send for me."

The woman looked at her with an expression Cherry could not decipher. Was it fear? The dignity of her bearing became steeliness, tension.

"Unless"—Cherry hesitated and urged again—"you'd like me to drop in, say, once a week, to see how you are getting along. Mondays would be good. Would Mondays suit you?"

"It isn't a question of Monday or Tuesday or Friday," Mary Gregory brushed her aside. But she faltered under Cherry's earnest gaze. "You say you—won't be back at all after tomorrow?"

"Unless you change your mind. I'd like to come back." And Cherry put into her eyes and voice all the concern she felt for this drifting woman.

Suddenly Miss Gregory turned a stricken face to Cherry and held out her hands. "Don't go away and never come back! Don't leave me all alone!"

Cherry could hardly believe her ears. She took a step forward. Mary Gregory burst out weeping.

"I've been wanting to—get back in touch—Wanting to for a long time now—But I don't know how—with people—And then you came, you're easy to talk to, you didn't ask me questions. But now you're leaving—Oh, help me, help me!"

Cherry took the woman's hand. She said very low, "I'll help you. I won't leave you."

She let the woman weep stormily, clinging to her hand. Years of dammed-up emotion overflowed at last. The tears were washing away the mental locks and bolts, so that finally Cherry could reach her. Cherry watched the racked woman with pity, until her sobs subsided.

"I'm—so ashamed, nurse."

"You needed to cry. Here, wipe your eyes. Take a sip of water." Cherry comforted her, smiled, sat down in a chair beside her. "Better now?"

"Yes, much better. Nurse, I wish—Would you let me talk to you? Would you listen? If you're going to help me—come back, I'd better tell you what's happened."

Cherry soothed her and reassured her. She settled back to listen, marveling at the change that had come over Mary Gregory in these last few minutes. The strain had slipped from her face, leaving it naked-looking, and her bearing was no longer steely but exhausted. She began to talk in low, rapid tones, not looking at Cherry.

Mary Gregory had been the only child of wealthy, elderly parents. They lived very much to themselves, and when a daughter was born to them, late in life, they kept their treasure to themselves. Mary Gregory was not permitted to go to school but was educated by private tutors at home. She traveled much with her parents, all over the world, throughout her childhood and adolescence. Rarely did she know other children, never did she have friends of her own age. She was constantly with her parents, and when occasionally she met other people, either they were much older than herself or Mary was strictly chaperoned and soon whisked away.

"You can see"—the woman looked at Cherry apologetically—"why I grew up fantastically shy and totally unable to deal with people. Oh, I like people, I wanted so much to know them and be friends with them. But my shyness held me back. There was only one person my own age to whom I ever felt close. Louise and I didn't see each other often, but we exchanged long letters when we were apart and we were dear friends. I liked writing to her sometimes better than seeing her face to face. I always had my mother and father, whom I loved dearly, for companionship. There seemed to be no need for other people. I suppose—I suppose I was a very odd sort of girl."

"Through no fault of your own," Cherry put in gently.

"You would think, wouldn't you, that the odds against my meeting a young man would be very great? Yet it happened. He was Louise's cousin, and he called on us—a purely polite call when we happened to be in San Francisco one year. I fell in love with him and—I was so grateful!—he with me. I was—rather pretty, then."

A ghost of tenderness flickered across Mary Gregory's face, as she sat remembering her love affair of long ago.

Reluctantly Mary Gregory's parents acceded to the courtship and gave permission for her marriage. John Wheeler was a handsome, robust, high-spirited young man, sociable and easygoing, the opposite of the shy girl who was to be his wife. "He was exactly the right temperament to draw me out of my shell," Miss Gregory murmured, smiling. "Everything I did in his company magically became easy, happy, thrilling—I forgot to be afraid of people when I could hear John laughing. He was so proud of me when he introduced me to his friends, and I felt free for the first time in my life. We planned to go all over the world together—he was an engineer and had to travel—"

Her face convulsed. She swiftly rose and went to a dresser. Opening the top drawer, she took out a small, white satin box and brought it over to Cherry. Shining in the box was an unworn wedding ring.

"Mrs. John Wheeler, I was to have been," Mary Gregory whispered. Weeping, she told Cherry the rest.

A month before their marriage, John had been called away on an engineering project. He would be back soon, he cheerfully told her to go ahead with the myriad preparations for their wedding. Mary Gregory was having the final fitting of her bridal gown, standing in the seamstress' dressing room in white satin and lace, when the telegram came. John Wheeler had been seriously injured in a construction accident. He was asking for her.

"My father did not want me to go, because John was in a little mountain village miles from anywhere, difficult of access. My mother was undecided. You can't imagine how I pleaded, when every minute counted! Finally, we rushed down by train and then had to go on by rented car. When we got there"—Mary Gregory choked—"it was too late. John had died alone. Asking for me."

She covered her face with her hands. She was barely able to go on. Cherry's heart swelled with pity for her, and for young John Wheeler dying alone in the alien mountains.

"You won't believe this." Mary Gregory looked up vaguely. She gripped the arms of her chair, the wedding ring in her lap. "My parents had dragged me from the crude hospital. I was half hysterical with grief. We started on our way back to the railroad in that rented car. Mountain roads—you know what they are, steep, narrow, hairpin curves, valleys miles below. It was night, and raining. And—our car plunged over the side."

Mary Gregory was in the hospital for months afterwards. It was feared she would never walk again. She kept asking for her parents. Why didn't they come to her? Finally the hospital people told her.

"I was left utterly alone. The three people I loved most were gone. The rest of the world, even Louise, seemed strangers to me. And after what had happened, I felt shyer, more terrified and crushed than ever. I—I just couldn't start out to face people, all over again, all by myself. I couldn't do it, I tell you! I couldn't do it!"

Some pitiful instinct to find a place of refuge led her back to this house, where as a very young child she had spent happy summers. Opening it up and finding all the dear, remembered things seemed to bring back her parents and their warm, safe, protective presence.

"I knew it was cowardly to run away and hide," Mary Gregory said gropingly. "I realized I was trying to return to my childhood, and that was wrong. But I wanted only to die, or to disappear."

Here in this house she had stopped all the clocks at quarter to three, the hour of her parents' death. The downstairs rooms were left as her parents would have wished them, and perversely it comforted her. Her own childhood bedroom, too, she had kept unchanged, standing in its aura of memories. The house was peopled with friendly ghosts, shedding the faint perfume of a happier time.

"Of John's things I had nothing but this ring, and a photograph of him. I had his portrait painted from that picture, and portraits of my parents. Then I hung them at the stair landing, so that I could imagine"—Mary Gregory smiled sadly—"they were downstairs, moving around in the familiar rooms, right here in the house with me."

"But upstairs—" Cherry was puzzled. "Upstairs, at least in your bedroom and sitting room, you are living in the present. Your furniture, what I've seen of your clothes, your radio and books, are quite new." She wondered, too, how Miss Gregory managed these things without ever leaving her house. "And I couldn't help seeing all those letters—"

Mary Gregory haltingly explained. She knew it was dangerous to shut herself away and that to retain her sanity, she must keep in touch with the outside world. More, though lacking courage to deal with people face to face, she wanted keenly to know them, at least through letters. Then, too, she felt guilty and selfish at using her wealth only for herself.

So—indirectly, through her bank and her attorney, never releasing this address to anyone else—Mary Gregory had played Lady Bountiful. Whenever she read of a worth-while welfare fund, particularly if children needed help, she wrote to them and contributed. Gradually she established a wide and vital correspondence. She had kept up with the news by ordering newspapers delivered through Mr. Jonas. She had bought books and a radio and house furnishings and even up-to-date clothes from department stores. All this had been done by mail (the postman picked up her outgoing letters from a box fastened beside her door) and the bank had handled all bills and money matters.

"So you see," Miss Gregory smiled, "I am of the world, though not in it."

She had read and studied a great deal. She spent hours every day keeping her house immaculate, cooking, making these fine embroideries which she loved, sewing for organizations for needy persons.

"I tried every sort of needlework I could think of. In the past year and a half, I even made these hooked rugs you see on the floor"—Cherry glanced down, noticing them for the first time—"and I still hook rugs occasionally."

"It's quite a task," said Miss Gregory, warming to her subject. "You need a big frame and a big hook. I experimented and devised a frame out of those large, wooden, curtain stretchers. Then I set the frame sideways to the window for a good light—though often I work at night, too, with a very strong light. You know, the threads hang down on the wrong side and I have to run from one side to the other." She added, smiling, "I'm light on my feet and dancing from side to side of that frame is good exercise."

"Then—that's what the children—" Cherry started but quickly silenced herself.

"I beg your pardon?"

Cherry was thinking that this, then, was the innocent explanation of the "witch's shadows" and the "gallows" which the soda fountain boy had fearsomely described. Of course! The strong light had silhouetted the curtain stretchers and Miss Gregory's active figure against the window. Bogeyman, indeed! Cherry determined to spread this true story as early and widely as possible.

"I was always busy," Miss Gregory summed up. "I tried not to give myself time to be lonely. But I was lonely. It's only in the past two years that I've come to admit it."

Cherry leaned forward, stirred by the strange story.

"Miss Gregory, haven't you anyone—any family—anyone at all?"

"No," she said. "There is really no one close to me except Louise Carewe. Louise and I have kept on writing to each other through the years. She lives in Thornwood where her husband was manager of a small store until his death. The last time I saw Louise," Mary Gregory reminisced, "she was a young girl. She came to tell me how happy she was that I was to be John's wife. She loved John, too. She named her boy for him."

Cherry thought she saw an opening here, a ray of hope. "Does she have more than one child?"

"Yes, she has a girl, too," Miss Gregory said warmly. "Louise sends me snapshots of them, to show me how they are growing up. I almost feel they are *my* children, too." She hesitated, then added delicately, "When Louise's husband died he left her almost nothing. I have been assisting financially, so her children may have a few more advantages."

"Then you do have a family!" Cherry said happily.

"Yes, I—I care very much for Louise and her two children."

"Then Louise would be the very person you'd want to see."

The effect of Cherry's words was like that of tossing a glass of cold water in the recluse's face. She paled and shrank back in her chair.

"Oh, no, no—I couldn't actually see her! I couldn't venture face to face. Letters, at a safe distance, are one thing, but to—"

"But you said you wanted to 'come back'!" Cherry cried.

Mary Gregory wearily drew her hand across her forehead. "I do want to. But I don't know whether I'll actually be able to do it. It will be an ordeal. I won't know what to say. I'll draw back, and Louise will be offended—"

"No, you won't, Miss Gregory," Cherry soothed. "Louise is no stranger to you, and she must love you for all you've done for her and her children."

"I haven't the courage." Her voice dropped. "No, I can't do it, after all."

Cherry pleaded, reasoned, reassured. Miss Gregory mutely shook her head and sat there trembling.

"I can't. I can't. It's too late."

There was only one way left. Cherry took a deep breath.

"Miss Gregory, you trust me, don't you? Will you tell me Louise's address?"

"She lives in Thornwood. Mrs. Donald Carewe— Why? Oh, Miss Ames, you mustn't—"

"Ssh, now. You know I wouldn't do anything that could possibly hurt you."

The woman looked up at her with pleading eyes. It was the same pathetic expression as when Cherry had first found her. It seemed to Cherry that, now as then, she was pleading to be rescued from her self-imposed prison. Her resistance and fears were automatic by now and less urgent than the pain in her eyes.

Out of that house, and out on the street again, with night falling and all this to figure out, the last person Cherry wanted to see was Driver Smith. Yet it was his bus she boarded.

As she stood beside him and opened her purse for fare, he favored her with a mock-elaborate nod.

"So it's the smart nurse! Good evenin', mado-moozelle, I'm tickled pink to see yah."

Cherry's too-quick temper rose at this taunt. But she decided to take it as a joke.

"Sir, I am tickled red, white, and blue to see you. I've missed you like anything."

He looked at her uncertainly, ready in his turn to grow angry. But he caught the merriment in Cherry's eyes.

"Y'know, lady, it kills me t' hafta take yer nickel."

They grinned at each other, for the first time. The bus started off. Cherry took a seat right behind Driver Smith and said practically into his ear:

"You're so charming these days, Mr. Smith, I'd gladly pay a dime to ride on your bus."

"Chawmin', she says. Lady, you ain't kidding! You think I can't be chawmin'? Huh! Watch this."

The bus slowed down and stopped at the next corner. A woman climbed aboard. She fished for a long time in her purse.

"Take yer time, lady," Driver Smith said, with only the slightest edge in his voice. "I wouldn' hurry ya for the world."

The woman smiled delightedly. "You certainly are the nicest bus driver I've met in a long time! Here you are."

"Oh, thank you, lady." Driver Smith was goggle-eyed at her reaction but he went on with his act. "Take a seat. Any seat you like."

The woman giggled and sat down. The other passengers who had overheard were smiling, too. As the bus started off again, Cherry hissed mockingly into Smith's ear:

"Didn't turn out quite the way you meant it to, did it?"

Driver Smith hissed back indignantly, "And why shouldn' people like me? So what's wrong with me? I can be chawmin' again, I betcha. Watch this!"

Corner after corner, Driver Smith was charming. He seemed astounded that he could actually play the part, and delighted with the novelty of it. Loudly enough for everyone to hear and appreciate him, he intoned:

"Step right in, mister, we been waitin' for yah!" "Glad t' see yah, lady, sorry yah hafta get off now." "So long, nurse, it wuz chawmin' havin' yah aboard."

Cherry left the bus giggling and wondering how long this transformation would last.

CHAPTER XII

A Welcome Guest

SATURDAY BROUGHT DECEMBER'S FIRST SNOW FLURRY and a small avalanche of mail for Cherry. She had to retreat with it into her and Gwen's bedroom, because the Spencer Club was in an uproar. The girls had collected dozens of Christmas dolls, which now populated the living room, and were debating mobilizing their districts' small boys, to build Christmas toys at Laurel House.

"Cherry Ames, you come right back here!" Gwen demanded with a toss of her red mane.

"I agree to everything," Cherry said hastily. "G'bye."

"Now, Cherry," Vivian gently reproved. "What are we going to do about doll clothes? We can't sew all of them ourselves."

"Have the little girls make some of 'em at Laurel House, maybe, and we'll make some. Look, kids,"

Cherry pleaded, "I have Mary Gregory's affairs to straighten out, I'm going to see Evelyn Stanley about food for the Christmas party, and I'm longing to read this mail. Please just assign me some tasks and I'll do my share, whatever you say."

"Fair enough," Bertha Larsen mumbled, her mouth full of pins as she adjusted Josie's hem. "Turn, Josie. And stand still!"

Mai Lee was too busy gluing doll wigs into place to say anything at all. Cherry escaped into the bedroom and bounced down on the bed with her pile of letters.

They all said much the same thing. Her mother wrote: "Are you coming home for Christmas and your birthday? We want so much to see you. Charlie is home nearly every week end, and we wish you weren't so far away." Midge enclosed proofs of some pictures of herself which would soon appear in the school paper. "Snappy? I'll never live down the funny one. I've been elected chairman of the nominating committee. Aren't you ever coming home?" And from the State University, Charlie scrawled: "Hi, twin! Our joint birthday, the 24th, and Christmas, the 25th, are getting close. We haven't had a birthday party together for too long. Meet me at home?"

She had no time to daydream over her mail, for the doorbell rang. It was a telegram for Miss Cherry Ames, sent en route from the Tucson–New York train:

Your House Two Saturday Afternoon Love Love Love Love Love—Wade.

Cherry let out a shriek. "And my hair isn't fixed, and my best dress is at the dry cleaner's!"

She raced into the living room, cheeks crimson, waving the telegram.

"Wade Cooper's coming! This afternoon! You've got to help me!"

The girls grinned. "She means curl her hair, get these dolls out of the way, and then try and make this place look presentable before Wade gets here."

"Yes," Cherry stammered. "I mean no! I mean—Vivi, for heaven's sake, will you give me a manicure? Right away?"

The Spencer Club hooted and teased. But they loyally provided beauty aids, a hasty house cleaning, and whisked the dolls away to the back parlor.

"Frankly," Gwen sighed two hours later, dabbing Cherry with perfume, "I wish the handsome ex-Captain Cooper thought *I* was purty."

"Silly," Cherry retorted. "Wade's true love is planes and you know it. Ouch! This zipper is stuck!"

By two o'clock Cherry was transformed from a sober nurse into her usual lively, vivid self. Wade liked bright colors, so she wore her red wool dress. Her cheeks and lips were nearly as brilliant, and her eyes glowed midnight black.

"You look like a red and black poster," Vivian said.

"I feel like a reconverted—Oh! The doorbell!"

The other girls scampered out of the living room. Cherry pulled open the blue door. A broad, navy broadcloth back faced her, as Wade stared bewildered out on the street.

"This Village place is plumb crazy!" he muttered.

Then Wade turned. He was tall and husky, and brown as could be—brown hair, brown eyes, handsome face tanned by sun and wind. He grinned at Cherry, and pumped her hand until it ached.

"Cherry! It sure is good to see you!"

Cherry smiled up at him, delighted to see her old friend and ex-pilot. "I never was better and how are you?"

Wade was all dressed up for this call in navy-blue suit, white shirt, red tie. Cherry was touched at the care he had taken. He strode into the living room, which suddenly looked smaller with this big lad in it, and thrust a beribboned box into Cherry's hands.

"Here. Candy. Who's the crazy bird who pestered me at the door?"

"Sam, our janitor, without a doubt. Wade, what a beautiful box. Thank you, thank you!"

"Never mind the box, stuff's inside. Isn't that just like a girl?—the box! Say, I met a barefoot man with a beard and a woman with a baby tiger, coming over here. What kind of crazy place is this Greenwich Village?"

His brown face crinkled into a smile. For a few seconds, he and Cherry just sat and beamed at each other. Then Wade told her he would be in New York for several days. "I'm staying with some fellows, fliers. Have to do some buying here for my business, and a couple of errands for my dad. But I'm saving plenty of time for you, Cherry. You'd better have time for me! Otherwise," he looked her squarely in the eye and pulled her curls, "I'll come along on your job with you."

"All dressed up in a blue nurse's uniform?" Cherry giggled. "My assistant? What a nice assistant! But I do plan to go up to Thornwood tomorrow to see a Mrs. Carewe if I can arrange an appointment with her—I must phone her. It's about an hour by train. Want to come along for the ride?"

"Sure thing. You're not going to run out on me, my first Sunday here. Say, will you please open that candy?"

Cherry untied the bow, while Wade tried to look nonchalant.

"Oh! Wade! These are the most gorgeous chocolates! How sweet of you."

They ate several chocolates and visited for a while. Then Cherry asked Wade to excuse her while she tried to reach Mrs. Carewe via long distance.

While she waited for the call to be completed, Cherry peered anxiously down the hall. Muffled voices and bangings came from the rear rooms. She hoped the girls weren't plotting any mischief.

"Hello?" a woman's voice said.

"Mrs. Carewe? Mrs. Louise Carewe? This is a nurse who has been taking care of your friend, Mary Gregory."

Cherry heard a gasp at the other end of the wire.

"Yes, she's all right. No, no, please don't worry. But I want to talk to you about her. . . . Yes, I'd be glad to come to your house, Mrs. Carewe. . . . Tomorrow afternoon at three would be perfect. . . . I'm Miss Ames, Cherry Ames. . . . Until tomorrow, then. Good-bye."

Wade, with his mouth full of chocolates, popped a chocolate into Cherry's mouth.

"Why are we going where're we going tomorrow afternoon?"

"This is a funny, sad sort of situation, Wade. I've decided the only solution is for me to take action, because nobody else will—or can. My supervisor at the center gave permission."

Cherry started to tell Wade a little about the recluse. The young man's eyes lost their mischief. At that point, Josie wandered in.

"Has anyone seen my pearl necklace?" Josie inquired transparently. She was wearing it. "Oh, hello, Wade."

Wade stood up, and shook hands.

Gwen burst in, one roguish eye cocked on Cherry.

"I'm sorry but—well, I just had to say hello to Wade!"

She pumped his hand and looked admiringly at the handsome young man.

"Good to see you, Red," he said warmly. "I always did like those cute freckles. Been taking good care of Cherry for me?"

Gwen made a face at him, then moaned: "Look at that candy! Too beautiful to eat—or is it?"

"Have some," Cherry said. "You, too, Josie. Why not call in the others?"

"Good idea," said Wade wanly.

Vivian, Mai Lee, and Bertha came in, all smiles, to greet Cherry's guest. Wade bore up bravely in the midst of six chattering girls.

"Cherry, we need your help with the dolls. Of course, this afternoon with Wade here—But how about your helping this evening?"

Wade announced: "I'm taking Cherry to the theater this evening. Sorry."

"Wade!" Josie squealed. "Come and see our dolls!"

"Me and dolls?" The flier squirmed. "Uh—thanks, anyhow."

But the girls pounced on Josie's suggestion and insisted that Wade see their collection and their handiwork. They shepherded him down the hall. Cherry's efforts to rescue him did no good. She followed them, giggling, into the back sitting room.

As the girls held up one doll after another before him, Wade looked bored and then scared. He glanced desperately around, as if seeking a means of escape.

Cherry was just opening her mouth to make a second rescue attempt when Bertha Larsen said:

"Wade, *you* could help with the dolls."

"Me? Fix up dolls?" Wade was outraged. "The idea!"

"You could at least paste on doll wigs," Gwen pointed out reasonably.

"Now see here, Red—if you think you're going to press me into service—Dolls!" He tried to bolt for the door but Bertha blocked the way.

"In fact," Vivian said, straight-faced, "Wade could even help with the doll clothes."

"I could not!"

He looked wildly toward Cherry for help, but Cherry had dissolved into silent, helpless laughter.

The doorbell rang, three short rings. Josie ran to answer, and came back in a moment with Dr. Johnny.

"Wade Cooper, Dr. John Brent." The two young men shook hands. "Johnny," said Josie plaintively, "will you help us with the dolls?"

"Sure," said the young doctor. "What do you want me to do? Take out their appendices?"

"No. Help make doll clothes."

"Uh—well—" Dr. Johnny grinned. "All right."

Wade stared at him. "You'll really do it?"

"I don't think it will hurt a bit," said the imperturbable Johnny. "No reason why a man shouldn't know how to sew or cook or mind a baby, is there?" And he settled down to pulling out basting threads.

There was not much Wade could do after that—to Cherry's huge amusement—but follow Dr. Brent's example. The sight of big Wade with a doll in one fist and a length of ruffle clenched in the other—Cherry had to bite her lips to keep from laughing aloud.

After about five minutes of diligent struggle with a needle, Wade looked up. "This whole process," he said gravely, "is inefficient."

"We haven't a sewing machine," Bertha replied.

"I mean the whole idea of sewing these little costumes is slow and inefficient. I just thought of a way that will save a lot of trouble on some of the doll dresses."

"What is it?" all the girls demanded. "We'd certainly be glad to speed up this job." Dr. John looked interested, too.

"Model airplane glue," said Wade. "It sticks like iron and we can glue some of the costumes together instead of sewing them."

"Triumph!" they acclaimed him.

Wade rushed out and returned a few minutes later with the special glue. It worked. By now Wade was so interested that he worked along all afternoon.

At dinner in a Village restaurant, at a table for two, Wade relaxed.

"I like your nurses, Cherry, honestly. But so many of 'em at once!"

"You did handsomely," Cherry congratulated him.

"Well, we have the whole evening ahead of us. Just you and me, Cherry." His brown face crinkled. He showed her a pair of theater tickets. "Ticket seller swore these were good seats. If they are, you've got to let me hold your hand!"

Arriving at the theater, it became clear that the ticket seller had spotted the tall, sunburned flier as an unsuspecting out-of-towner. Cherry's seat was on one side of a massive pillar, and Wade's seat was on the other side, a good four feet away.

Sunday, Wade telephoned Cherry and they met at a restaurant near Grand Central Station for lunch. Cherry loved the place Wade chose. "You're the perfect escort," she smiled at him.

"We aim to please," Wade said cheerfully. "What's all this about a mysterious shut-in and Mrs. Carewe?"

Cherry finished telling him the story, briefly. She was curious about what Louise Carewe might be like, and not a little worried.

By the time they boarded the train for Thornwood, Cherry was so distracted that Wade said:

"Now stop that! You've done everything you can, to this point. Worrying won't make it any better."

He drew Cherry's attention to himself, telling her why he did not care much for the auto repair business.

"Too tame. Course, I like engines and speed, but I like 'em in a plane. I'm going back into flying first chance I get. Maybe while I'm here in New York I can line up a pilot's job. Bill and Terry, two of the fellows I'm staying with, are commercial pilots."

"Good luck, Wade," Cherry breathed. "Auto repair does sound too safe and sane for you. Haven't you been in any breakneck scrapes lately?"

Wade grinned. "Sure. Took up a neighbor's private plane last week and put on the best exhibition of stunt flying Tucson's seen in a dog's age. Then my dad bawled me out for being wild. The neighbor was scared half to death." Wade chuckled. "He was in the plane, nose diving with me."

He told her the hair-raising details. By this time the train was pulling into Thornwood. They got off and found themselves in a pretty little town with neat houses and churches. Wade said he would wait here at the station for Cherry.

"This visit won't take awfully long," Cherry said.

Wade put her in a taxi. She gave Mrs. Carewe's address. The taxi took her through the center of town and then along quiet streets lined with modest homes.

They drew up before a salt-box type of house. Cherry paid her fare and stepped out.

Mrs. Carewe was waiting for her at the door. She was a gracious person, still pretty, but weary-looking. She was on crutches and one leg was in bandages. With her was her daughter, a girl of eighteen, also named Louise. She looked startlingly as her mother must have looked at her age. Cherry also met the son, a pleasant boy of about fourteen.

They went into the little living room. Cherry saw a youthful photograph of Mary Gregory on the mantel. The three women sat down together and there was a strained pause. Since Mrs. Carewe seemed rather agitated, Cherry opened the conversation.

"Mrs. Carewe, I have an amazing story to tell you, but a hopeful story," Cherry began. She outlined all that had happened between Mary Gregory and herself. Then she told what had gone on in the recluse's house, and in the recluse's mind, all these years. Mrs. Carewe and her daughter Louise listened in tense silence.

When Cherry finished, Mrs. Carewe's eyes were wet.

"I'd do anything in the world to help her," she said earnestly. "I remember Mary Gregory as a beautiful and pathetic young woman. She was so shy and strange. Now you say her hair is gray! Her letters have always been full of other things besides herself all these years, of course. . . . What can I do?" she begged.

"See her. That is the first step. *If* she will see you."

"But Mary knows I love her. Surely she—"

"It isn't as simple as that, Mrs. Carewe." Cherry looked at her. It was a relief to find her, and her daughter, too, kind and understanding people. But could Miss Gregory be persuaded to see her? And even if an interview was managed, it might fail or disastrously drive

Mary Gregory still deeper into her shell. Still, it had to be tried, risk or no risk. Then Mrs. Carewe said something that complicated matters.

"The trouble is I can't travel, nor even leave my house, with this fractured leg. You see, I slipped and fell on an icy walk. I won't be able to get down to New York for a long while." She hesitated. "I feel dreadfully sorry not to be able to go—after Mary's generosity to us!

She has been wonderfully kind. And now, just when she needs me—"

This was a bad disappointment. Cherry looked speculatively at the daughter. Young Louise must be the image of her mother as she was the last time Mary Gregory saw her.

"Could your daughter go?"

"Oh, yes, yes," both women exclaimed. Young Louise said that she felt she knew and loved the recluse as much as her mother did.

"Miss Ames, when may I go to her house? Soon?" the girl asked.

Cherry reflected. "It might be wiser not to tell her you are coming. Not give her a chance to worry beforehand and build up all sorts of defenses. Let's say, Miss Carewe, that you'll go in with me when I make another routine nursing visit."

They set a date for the coming week. Young Louise looked very thoughtful and troubled. "I may not know what to say," she confessed. "You'll have to engineer that meeting, Miss Ames, if Aunt Mary's whole future depends on it."

Cherry sighed. "We'll both do the best we can."

Driving back to the station, she reflected on how to handle this meeting.

"Whew!" Wade whistled when Cherry told him about her visit. "That's a fine, explosive problem you have on your hands."

"Want to take over on the Gregory case?" Cherry teased.

"No! But I'll tell you what I would like to do." He grinned, looking like a happy six-year-old. "Ask me what."

"What?" Cherry asked obligingly.

"Go to the Central Park zoo, when we get back to the city, with you. Go to dinner, with you. Go to the Aviation Show, with you. Spend the rest of the evening dancing, with—"

"I get the idea, Wade, and it sounds wonderful."

They spent the balance of Sunday doing Wade's program. Giraffes, man-sized steaks, and planes took Mary Gregory off Cherry's mind temporarily. Half the fun, as Wade said, was that just the two of them were having this romp. Wade took a tremendous number of taxis, even for two blocks, "because taxis and you are my idea of The Works."

The evening grew late and later, but Wade and Cherry paid no attention. On Fifty-first Street, the two of them stopped in at a roller-skating rink for a brisk whirl around the huge, wood floor. Eleven o'clock found them dancing dreamily in a great hotel ballroom. At twelve they were perched on stools at a hamburger counter. At one o'clock Cherry and Wade stood on No. 9's doorstep, tired but happy.

"It was divine," Cherry said.

"Wasn't it? But no more doll dressing!"

"You didn't care for it?" Cherry teased. "A fine assistant you turned out to be."

"Nevertheless I'm going to remain your assistant all the time I'm here!"

Wade strode off down the moonlit Greenwich Village street, whistling.

CHAPTER XIII

The Test

CHERRY COULD THINK OF NOTHING BUT MARY GREGORY and what was to become of her. The critical hour was at hand, and she must take on the heavy responsibility of Mary Gregory's encounter with the past—and the future. Even with Wade Cooper in town—even with excited preparation for Christmas and the settlement house party—even though her feet practically tap-danced over her snowbound district, with the season's approaching gaiety—still, an undercurrent of anxiety gripped Cherry.

A visit to Laurel House on her lunch hour helped dispel that. Evelyn Stanley greeted her with "It's all coming true! Come here and see for yourself!" That lively young woman seized Cherry's hand and drew her to the open doors of the craft shops.

Seated around a huge table, which was laden with the Spencer Club and other donors' dolls, and with piles of colorful remnants, ribbons, laces, doll shoes, little girls were busily sewing doll clothes. The tiny dresses and bonnets were so tastefully designed, so darling, that Cherry regretted she was not several years younger.

The sewing instructor glanced up with a smile. "You visiting nurses may have some of these dolls to distribute to your sick patients. The Girl Scouts will wrap them. The rest of the dolls will go under the Laurel House Christmas tree. How do you like Susie Belle?"

Susie Belle was a southern belle doll, in ruffled crinolines and poke bonnet. There was a bride doll, a farmer-boy doll, a Spanish doll with lace mantilla, and so many others that Evelyn Stanley had to pry Cherry away from that studio.

"Don't overlook the boys! Doesn't this look like old Kris Kringle's workshop?"

Cherry peered into the carpentry workshop. Nearly thirty young boys were hard at work, turning lathes, hammering, gluing, measuring. Under their capable hands, toys were taking shape: kites, precision construction sets, model planes, scooters, wagons, hobby horses and blocks for the very small fry.

"Like this, Philip," said a man's singsong voice. "Use your T square, measure so, allow for the joining—"

"Uncle Gustave!" Cherry exclaimed.

Gustave Persson got up stiffly from the workbench, dusted off his hands on his denim apron, and shook hands with Cherry. The little man's eyes were bluer, and his expression more contented, than Cherry had ever seen them.

"Uncle Gustave consented to become one of our carpentry instructors," Miss Stanley explained. "He volunteers his services, and he is so good we are only afraid someone will steal him away from Laurel House."

"I would not go," Uncle Gustave said stoutly. "I build you the Music School next. In the spring. Soon I make the blueprints."

"Congratulations to both of you!" said Cherry.

In the next studio, older boys and girls on ladders were building and painting stage scenery. The immense, cardboard slides depicted a beach and ocean, a farm kitchen, and a carnival. There was a great bustle in here, with everyone in overalls or smocks, and smudged with paint—including Cherry's quiet Miss Culver. Cherry was astonished.

"Why, Miss Culver! I didn't dare hope you'd be strong again this soon! I'm so glad to see you here."

Miss Culver sat down demurely on her ladder. "How nice to see you, Miss Ames. Miss Stanley called on me and invited me to the painting class. Then I saw this studio, and they did need extra hands. Isn't it nice?"

A distinguished, older man appeared at the doorway, unbuttoning his overcoat. He bowed slightly to Miss Culver and greeted Evelyn Stanley.

"Miss Ames," the social worker said, "this is Mr. Kenneth Long, the painter. Mr. Long gives painting instruction at Laurel House once a week. He is an Academy member and we are very proud to have him."

The painter acknowledged the introduction and looked at Cherry with special interest. "So you are the nurse who indirectly brought Miss Culver into my class. Come in here, please. You must see her work. I'm quite interested."

He went off ahead. Evelyn Stanley whispered to Cherry as they followed him:

"I don't know whether Mr. Long is more interested in Emily Culver's paintings or in Miss Emily herself."

"A romance?" Cherry gasped delightedly.

"I wouldn't be at all surprised. They are excellent friends. Ssh."

The painter was waiting for them in the studio. He had stood up against the easels several canvases, still lifes and landscapes. They were simple and naïve in technique, but their color was fresh as a sampler and they were patterned with the exquisite orderliness of Miss Culver herself. Cherry recognized two street scenes, painted from those second-floor windows, one at noon, one at dusk.

"Primitives, of course," Kenneth Long said, trying to

deprecate the pleasure in his voice, "but very nice. Very nice indeed. The entire class has talent, in some degree. Look at these others."

He spread out more canvases. Each one bespoke the individual who had painted it. Cherry was fascinated.

"Haven't you enough pictures there to"—she hesitated—"have an exhibition? At the Christmas party?"

Miss Stanley and the artist exchanged glances.

"An excellent idea," said Kenneth Long. "When can we hang them?"

Miss Culver, standing shyly in the doorway, looked as if she had seen her first rainbow.

In the auditorium was a man with the soberest face Cherry ever saw directing rehearsals of one of the funniest plays Cherry had ever heard.

"That's Mr. Twiddy," Evelyn Stanley whispered in her ear. "He wandered in here out of the blue with that sidesplitting play he wrote himself. And I've yet to see him crack a smile!"

Miss Stanley told Cherry the play would be produced for the party, and the party would be held a little before Christmas Day itself. Cherry was pleased at that, for she wanted to be home for her birthday and Christmas. "But I wouldn't miss this party for all the corn in Illinois!"

Then the two young women got down to business about an "Around The World" food table, or food bazaar. Cherry had already invited neighborhood people to cook their *kondis* and chicken broth with dumplings and *pasta* and lemon *tshay*—the well-to-do owner of a local cafeteria promised to supply the food provisions—and to play hosts as well. Everyone had eagerly accepted. But from all of them came insistence on having "American dishes too! We are Americans, Miss Ames! These other things belong to the past. Hot dogs, Miss Ames, and apple pie, and corn bread, please—that's what we want."

There was still a great deal to do, and still several days to go until the holiday. Meanwhile people were sick, Christmas or no Christmas, and Cherry had to make her calls. A severely burned hand to dress, a newborn baby whose mother needed instruction, a septic sore throat to irrigate, two cases of pneumonia. And Mary Gregory still to deal with . . . Wade teased on the telephone to accompany her, but Cherry knew better than to mix personal matters into business. Besides, the rules of the Visiting Nurse Service forbade anyone without official business to enter these homes.

Cherry regretted, however, that Wade could not meet Driver Smith. His play-acting at being pleasant had turned into the real thing.

"Glad to see ya!" he greeted Cherry. "Let the lady in! Ladies first! The war's over."

Cherry grinned and proffered her fare.

"Sorry I have t' charge ya," Smith told her.

As the bus rolled off, Driver Smith sang out, "We are now approachin' Jefferson Park, to yer right. Temperature is now thirty degrees, more'r less, humidity nine'y-two. Ya wanna get off, mister? Sure. Call again!"

This went on continuously, without a lull. Between welcomes to passengers, Driver Smith sang. The busload of people were a little startled, some of them were convulsed, but everybody enjoyed the ride.

"G'bye, nurse! Sorry t' see ya go. I thank ya for yer patronage!"

Cherry would have enjoyed all this a great deal more had not people begun to stop her on the street and ask questions. "Nurse, my neighbor saw you going into the Gregory house. Did she really let you in?" "Mr. Jonas told us Miss Gregory is sick and we should stay away from there, not bother her. But tell us, nurse, confidentially, what did you find out?" "I hear you've actually seen the poor soul. O'Brien won't tell a thing. What's she like?" Cherry wished she could say, "Mary Gregory is returning to the world." But that was still only a wish.

Most concerned of all were the children of the neighborhood. Cherry had told them the real story behind the scary legend they had built up in this past year or two. "Then she's really nice? After all?" "Poor thing, all alone." "Is she going to get well?" And the children gave Cherry notes and homemade Christmas presents and a spray of red berries to deliver to Miss Gregory. Despite

Officer O'Brien's vigilance, people were beginning to stand beside the fence of the Victorian mansion and stare into its masked windows.

Cherry was afraid that this might cost Mary Gregory whatever small courage she was mustering. Cherry particularly dreaded the possibility of real crowds gathering, of reporters and photographers, if some newspaper got wind of the story.

Cherry discussed her fears with Wade that evening at dinner. The two of them dined together so often that the Spencer Club jokingly warned Cherry that they no longer considered her an active member. And with ponderous tact, the girls avoided the Jumble Shop, Wade's favorite Village restaurant.

Wade and Cherry were squeezed in side by side on a banquette in the restaurant. Wade was "borrowing" bites of Cherry's dessert, having finished his own.

"Wade—I mean Cap'n—you've flown planes around the world. Do you think you could meet Louise Carewe's daughter at Grand Central Station and find the way out to the Gregory house, arriving in a nice, inconspicuous taxi?"

"I think so."

"Tomorrow, then." Cherry sat brooding. Tomorrow!

"You know what?" Wade remarked. "You're the prettiest girl in the room."

"You only think so. You're prejudiced."

"I certainly am, in your favor. Come on, let's go some place and dance."

They danced all evening, but Cherry's heart was not in it. For once, Wade, too, was ready to go home early. When he left her at No. 9, he said comfortingly, "Don't worry. Maybe tomorrow evening at this time we can celebrate about your Miss Gregory."

"Maybe," she murmured. "Maybe."

Next day Cherry took out the door key Miss Gregory had trustfully given her, and let herself in. She left the door unlatched for young Louise. The doorbell had been disconnected, so Cherry called, "Hello!" and started upstairs. She left certain bundles on the stair landing where the portraits were.

"Hello, Miss Gregory!" she called, climbing the rest of the stairs. "It's the nurse! How are you this fine day?"

Mary Gregory actually answered her. "Very well, thank you! Come in!"

Miss Gregory stood in the doorway of the upstairs sitting room. She was dressed in a modern frock but something about the cloudy lace scarf on her shoulders, and the timeless, madonna coiffure of her dark, silvered hair, gave her a remote look. Cherry glanced anxiously at her wrist watch, then said:

"This is a routine call. I hope you feel well enough to have visitors?"

"Oh, yes, I am fully recovered now. And I—I am glad to have a visitor, Miss Ames," she said with an effort.

With innate courtesy, Mary Gregory was trying to put Cherry at ease—which Cherry intended her to do.

"Then maybe you wouldn't mind having other visitors soon?" Cherry hinted. Mary Gregory's lips parted to protest. But Cherry, having planted the idea of visitors, gave her no chance to protest. She immediately went on talking casually of the children who had been asking for Miss Gregory, of their excitement at Christmas coming, of anything. More, Cherry got Mary Gregory to talking. "By the way, Miss Gregory, I want to return your door key. Here you are."

A low, sharp whistle sounded from downstairs. It was Wade. Miss Gregory turned, startled.

"That's for me," Cherry said, reassuring but not explaining. "Will you excuse me for a few moments?"

Now came the test! Cherry raced downstairs and met Wade and Louise Carewe in the kitchen. The young girl, in her hat and coat, carrying flowers, looked anxious and excited. Wade was distinctly uncomfortable. They conversed in whispers.

"Right on time! Wade, you stay down here. Miss Carewe, come with me." On the stair landing, Cherry piled young Louise Carewe's arms with bundles, again whispering. She called cheerfully, "Miss Gregory! Here are Christmas gifts for you!"

She urged the girl forward. Louise's eyes were apprehensive but she was smiling. Cherry followed a few paces behind.

"Gifts for me? From whom?" came Mary Gregory's astonished voice. Then Cherry heard her gasp: "Louise!"

"Gifts from"—the girl's voice broke and went on—"the neighborhood children. A few flowers. Oh, Aunt Mary!"

"Louise!" Mary Gregory was standing there, too shocked to move. Cherry, at young Louise Carewe's elbow, kept gently urging her forward. "Louise! It is the daughter, young Louise, isn't it?"

"Yes. Oh, Aunt Mary, Aunt Mary. I am so happy finally to see you! Mother couldn't come because she has fractured her leg—she is so sorry she cannot come, she longs to see you. But if you will accept me in her place temporarily—She and Brother send you all their love."

"I—I don't know what to say—I—" Mary Gregory burst into tears and hid her face in her hands. The young girl, too, had tears on her cheeks, but she smiled.

"No need to say anything." Cherry stepped in. "Here, let's go into the sitting room." She engineered the two tense women into the pleasant room.

"Why, Miss Gregory, aren't you going to open the children's gifts?" Cherry went on to fill the gap. "Come now, the youngsters are so eager to know if you like them."

Miss Gregory with shaking fingers began to untie the homemade presents. The young girl helped her. Having something to do together bridged the first embarrassment, and gave them something to talk about. After admiring the little gifts, Mary Gregory was able to look full at young Louise and managed to say:

"You look just as your mother did, when I last saw her. How is she?" Without waiting for an answer, she murmured, "So you are the little girl in the photographs, grown up now." Miss-Gregory smiled at the girl beside her.

"Aunt Mary, your letters have been wonderful. You've been so good to me and Mother and John. There is no way for us to thank you for your years and years of kindness."

Mary Gregory shrank back. Cherry quickly broke into the dangerous pause. "With Christmas and New Year's coming, this is really a good time for a family reunion, isn't it?"

Louise caught the cue. "Come and spend the holidays with us, Aunt Mary. Mother can't leave the house and she does so want to see you. Please, Aunt Mary?"

Mary Gregory hesitated, her whole figure taut.

"Of course she will," said Cherry, smiling encouragement at her.

"Of course I will," Mary Gregory echoed breathlessly. She sat up straighter and asked: "What ever became of Edward and Julia Weeks? Do you know, child?"

"They are living in New York. They write to Mother regularly and often mention you. They would love to see you."

"And—and do you ever go to the theater, Louise? I have missed the theater."

"You and Mother and I shall see whatever plays you like."

Cherry advised softly, "Set a date. Right now." The girl nodded. The older woman talked on, eagerly, of old times, old friends, while young Louise nodded that she understood. Cherry rose and tiptoed out of the room. She was at the door when Miss Gregory broke off to say:

"Miss Ames. Will you thank the children for me for their gifts?"

"Wouldn't you rather thank them yourself? They want to see you, they won't be satisfied with my word."

"Then"—Mary Gregory lifted her head and swallowed—"ask the children to a tea party, here. Sometime."

Cherry had to restrain a shout of joy. Mary Gregory was opening her doors at last! "Say this Saturday afternoon at three?" Cherry pinned her down.

"And I'll come down to help and keep order," Louise quickly put in.

"A tea party Saturday afternoon at three," Mary Gregory confirmed wonderingly. All at once she had become radiant. "Louise, bring your brother John—I want to see him. Give your mother my love and we will meet at Christmas, in—in Thornwood. And here is my door key, Louise, for you to—keep."

Cherry ran joyously downstairs. She found Wade striding stiffly around the hall.

"Wade! It worked! It worked!"

"Praise be! I sure have been sweating it out!"

From the kitchen Officer O'Brien and Mr. Jonas peered in excitedly. "It's all right? She's going to be all right?"

"Mary Gregory is going to lead a normal life from now on!" Cherry told them fervently. They mopped their brows in unison.

Cherry glowed. Her work and idealism as a nurse had truly served another human being. Her nurse's training had led her to this lonely soul, and had equipped her to save her.

She stood for a moment in the hall, gazing in at the three, silent, Victorian rooms. Then she turned to look at the grandfather's clock with its hands stopped at quarter to three.

"Wade, what time is it?"

"Twenty minutes past five."

Cherry stepped over to the tall clock and very deliberately opened its glass door. She urged the hands around to five-twenty, then gently started the pendulum swinging. Its cheerful ticking filled the hallway.

"Now my work here is done."

CHAPTER XIV

Christmas Party

THE CHRISTMAS PARTY WAS IN FULL SWING WHEN THE six nurses, Wade, and Dr. Johnny arrived at Laurel House, the Sunday before Christmas. The gymnasium had been transformed with fir boughs, and red and green decorations. In the center of the floor a Christmas tree towered almost to the ceiling, laden with dolls and toys from the workshops, with more dolls and toys spread under its sweeping branches. At one end of the crowded gym was the longest table Cherry had even seen, crammed with delicious foods and presided over by beaming, neighborhood hosts and hostesses. At the far end of the room, an orchestra of young people played at intervals. Evelyn Stanley, in her emerald-green dress and a glittering star in her hair, seemed to be everywhere at once.

She ran over to welcome the nurses and their visitors.

"We've been waiting for you! Miss Ames, the international food table is a wild success! And you'll never guess who's here! Mary Gregory."

"You're joking."

"I'm not joking. Look over there, in that crowd of children."

Cherry and Wade, the entire interested Spencer Club, turned. Across the room sat Mary Gregory, with young Louise Carewe at her side. Playing with the other children was Jimmy Terrell, now as good as new. Emily Culver, followed by Mr. Long's approving glance, was showing the Sergeyevskys the paintings that filled one big wall.

It seemed to Cherry that her entire district had come to the party—and many more, besides. Cherry spoke to the people she knew, sampled the goodies, with Wade attended a boxing contest between "underweights," helped run a game of musical chairs.

Then Cherry and Wade and the nurses adjourned with the others to the auditorium. There were so many guests that Mr. Twiddy's play had to be performed twice this afternoon, for two audiences. It was hilariously funny and the amateur players acted it with dash—except when a prop, a pretended wall safe, refused to open and deadpan Mr. Twiddy accidentally popped out from the wings clutching a hammer.

"It was a fine party," everybody agreed. "Let's have more parties at Laurel House. Especially with those delicious foods!" Cherry saw neighborhood people scribbling recipes and writing down one another's addresses, new acquaintances arranging to meet again. She felt warmly satisfied.

After that, it seemed to Cherry, Village characters, Wade, Christmas shopping, the Jenkinses, her packed suitcase, kaleidoscoped and whirled about her. She never quite understood how she managed to get safely to Grand Central Station. But here she was on the platform, heading midwest for her Christmas holiday, and Wade with his suitcase heading southwest. Their trains waited on either side of the long platform.

"Good-bye, honey," Wade said, surrounded by the Spencer Club. "Have a good birthday and Christmas. We'll get together soon again."

"Good luck, Wade!" Cherry glowed. "Thanks for the most wonderful time! So long, Gwen, Vivi. Mai Lee, make Vivian eat enough. Josie, Bertha, so long. Merry Christmas. Have fun!"

Wade put her aboard, finding her seat for her. She stood at the train window, looking out at the girls, and then at Wade waving and making faces from his window. The girls were motioning, trying to tell her something through the window, laughing helplessly. Then, simultaneously, the trains were moving.

Wade and Cherry waved to each other from their windows. The trains were slowly sliding along. The girls ran alongside, waving, slipping away one by one as the train picked up speed. Cherry waved frantically. Then Wade's train branched away, and he, too, was gone.

Cherry sat down in her Pullman seat and had to blow her nose, to her own surprise.

"I don't like saying good-bye, even for a little while." She tossed back her black curls. "But it'll be wonderful to see Mother and Dad and Charlie and home and everyone. And anyhow, I have lots and lots more nursing ahead of me!"